THE UNTOLD
STORY OF SEETA

THE UNTOLD STORY OF SEETA

her journey through fields,
palaces and forests

Neeraja Phatak

PARTRIDGE

A Penguin Random House Company

To order additional copies of this book, contact
Partridge India
000 800 10062 62
orders.india@partridgepublishing.com

www.partridgepublishing.com/india

For my mother

ACKNOWLEDGEMENTS

My grateful thanks to my mother Kusum Phatak for her unconditional support through my journey; to Anjani Singh in Pune who spared her valuable time reading endless versions of the manuscript, gently suggesting changes and patiently editing; to V. Krishna of Samata Books in Chennai for his encouragement and advice; to Issaikavi Venkateswaran for sharing with me over the years transcripts of my revered guru Sadguru K Sivananda Murty's talks; Guruji's words of wisdom and counsel have added depth to my story, without His blessings this book would not have seen the light of day.

A big thank you to Ananyaa Mital for the cover page.

Padma Narayan and Aditi Phatak thank you for your encouragement and belief in me; Devna Kamat and Nivedita Rao thank you for your suggestions and encouragement.

Last but not least, I'd like to thank Nelson Cortez and Gemma Ramos of Partridge Publishing for their support.

Author's Note

There was always a discordant note in the retellings of the Ramayana that I heard that have nagged me. How could Ram, regarded the best among all men publicly humiliate his wife in the name of 'Dharma'? How could Seeta the daughter of the great Janak accept this humiliation? Explanations came fast and thick – "Greatest good for the greatest number": "Giving up personal happiness for the good of society": "A wife's duty is to accept her husband wishes in the larger interests of society". These explanations did not convince me and I embarked on a journey looking for Seeta.

The Ram and Seeta I met were not merely formally wedded husband and wife, but they were companions. Under his composed exterior I discovered that Ram was a loving husband and a romantic man. The world lauded him for his adherence to his Dharma, be it as a son, brother, friend or King; but that he was often caught between a rock and a hard place was known only to his wife. As I followed her I was amazed at Seeta's sagacity and resilience. Their sons Luv and Kush became the Kings of Kosala not only because Ram was their father but because Seeta was their mother.

This narrative is in no way a retelling of the Ramayana; it describes situations in the Ramayana as I believe Seeta experienced them; other incidents essential to provide the context and keep the wholeness of the story, have been included.

Neeraja Phatak
Noida,
8 April 2014
Ramnavmi

Mahamahopadhyaya, Desikottama
Dr K. Sivananda Murty
D.Lit (GITAM Uni), D.Lit (PS Tel Uni)
Peethadhipati,
Sri Saiva Maha Peetham,

'Anandavan'
Bheemunipatnam
Visakha District
Andhra Pradesh - 531 163
Ph (08933) 229505
email:ksivanandamurty@gmail.com
Dt.29/05/2014

"The untold Story of Seeta" told for the first time by Ms Neeraja Phathak which makes a readable material. Any writer puts his or her own thoughts and words into the mouth of a classical character. Such literature abounds in all languages in the recent century. This write-up is Seeta's dairy .

Venkateswaran a brilliant journalist and a Tamil poet and a prolific writer(awaiting editing), has been with my family for long and Ms Neeraja mentions about his writings. This work will find its own liking readership. My Good wishes to Ms. Neeraja Phatak.

(k. Sivananda Murty)

CONTENTS

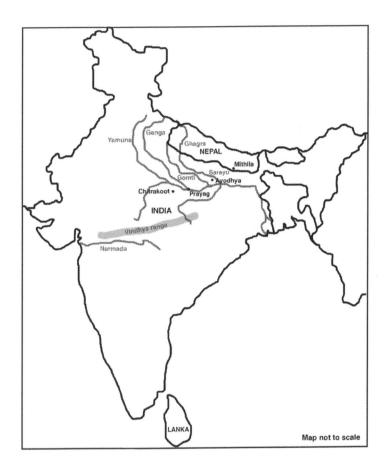

Map not to scale

CHAPTER 1
Early Years

Nestled in the southern foothills of the Himalayan Range in the Terai region[1] lay the kingdom of Videha with its capital Mithila, now known as Janakpur or 'the city of Janaks' in Nepal. The events that unfold occurred in the Treta Yuga[2] during the rule of Seeradhwaj Janak of the 'Videh Janak' dynasty. Seeradhwaj Janak was the most celebrated of the fifty two kings of the dynasty. He was referred to as merely 'Janak'. But, beyond the region, the dynasty is better known because of Seeta, the wife of Lord Ram who was the daughter of Seeradhwaj Janak and Queen Sunaina.

King Janak is remembered not only as a great king and warrior but as a wise and learned man, well versed in the

---

[1] Terai or grassy marshlands at the base of the outer Himalayas in the North of India and South of Nepal

[2] Yuga in Hindu philosophy is the name of an epoch or era within a four age cycle. One cycle of the four yugas – Satya also known as Krita, Treta, Dwapar and Kali makes one Mahayug. The Yuga on earth today is the Kali Yuga.

Vedic texts – a Raj-Rishi[3]. Rishi Yaagnavalkya who was known for his unsurpassed spiritual wisdom and power thought Janak a fit pupil and revealed to him 'Brahma Jnana' or knowledge of the creator. Janak invited to his court, men of learning who debated on the secrets of life and its creation. The Sage Ashtavakra also instructed Janak upon the nature of the self or Atman - this exposition forms the content of the famous treatise the 'Ashtavakra Gita'.

An interesting story about the birth of Sage Ashtavakra is that he was born 'wise and learned'; as he had absorbed the texts and the commentaries while in his mother's womb; and with eight deformities in his body. The deformities were a result of his father's curse; Ashtavakra means crooked (vakra) at eight (ashta) points. His parents were Rishi Kahod and Sujata. Rishi Kahod was very poor and was preparing to go to the court of Janak to participate in a theological debate in the hope that he would win the debate and be rewarded. He was chanting the mantras, as Sujata, pregnant with her child sat beside him. Rishi Kahod was inattentive and mispronounced some words; each time Rishi Kahod mispronounced a word, the foetus squirmed. After this had happened eight times, the foetus asked his father to be attentive to his chanting. Rishi Kahod was furious at the arrogance of the un-manifest form and cursed it, "You will be born crooked in as many places as the number of times you have wanted to correct your father." At Janak's court, Rishi Kahod was defeated by Rishi Bandi, another scholar; the rules of the debate dictated that the loser drown himself;

---

[3]   A sage amongst kings

accordingly Rishi Kahod met a watery death before his son was born.

As a child Ashtavakra would often ask his mother about his father. At first his mother fobbed off the question, but ultimately had to tell him the truth. When Ashtavakra learnt the truth he vowed to challenge 'Bandi' in a debate. He set off for Mithila, where a debate was in progress. As Ashtavakra hobbled into pavilion the wise participants and courtiers burst into laughter at the ungainly sight. Whereupon Ashtavakra himself began to laugh and almost collapsed in helpless laughter and then there was silence. King Janak asked Ashtavakra the cause of his laughter; "Oh King!" said Ashtavakra. "I thought this was a gathering of scholars, but I see they are mere cobblers – they judge a person on the basis of the skin". Again there was silence, this time an embarrassed silence as the courtiers hung their heads in discomfiture. The King then invited Ashtavakra to the debate and Ashtavakra defeated 'Bandi' but would not allow 'Bandi' to drown himself. "Knowledge," Ashtavakra said, "should be used for progress and not as a weapon".

One time the kingdom of Videha was reeling under a famine; the rains had failed for three consecutive years. If that year too the rains failed, there would not be enough food for the people. The level of grains in the royal granaries was steadily falling. Seeradhwaj Janak was worried about the distress of his people, how would they survive if the rains failed again? Their distress and despair was experienced by the King a hundred times over. The King had noted that the lines of people waiting to be served free food outside the palace gates were getting longer by the day. Gloom descended on the palace, meal times were the worst when despite pleas and entreaties from his queen Sunaina, Janak would barely eat a couple of morsels of food.

One morning the renowned Sage, Rishi Narada arrived at the Court in Mithila. Narada was known as Dev-Rishi[4] Narada. Deva-Rishis were sages who had complete understanding of the three lokas or the three worlds - the earth, the world of the ancestors and the world of the Gods. Rishi Narada's visit was a great honour and he was received with due respect, his feet were washed, and anointed with sandal wood paste and kumkum, by the King himself; the Sage was offered fruits and sweets and seated in a place of honour. In deference to the Sage's stature the King sat on a lower seat; and the two, the Deva-Rishi and Raj-Rishi were engaged in discussion on issues of life here and hereafter and the welfare of the kingdom. Both were worried about the coming of the Kali Yug which great Seers had predicted would be characterised by avarice and wrath, men would openly display animosity towards each other. Ignorance of Dharma would occur. Lust would be viewed as being socially acceptable. People would have thoughts of murder for no justification, and they would see nothing wrong with that mind-set. Rulers would be selfish and think only of their own good. Means would justify ends as 'Dharma' would be understood only as performing rituals and not as a code of ethics of doing one's duty in the true spirit of position held in the family, social or political context[5].

---

[4]   Sage among the Gods

[5]   Unpublished talks of Sadguru K Sivananda Murthy

During the course of the conversation Rishi Narada suggested that Janak perform a Yagna[6] which would bring relief to the famine stricken kingdom and help the King and his wife beget children. The Rishi narrated how a couple of years earlier the King of Kosala, King Dashrath of the Raghu Dynasty had performed a Great Yagna for begetting sons; and this had resulted in all three of his wives Kaushalya, Sumitra and Kaikeyi being blessed with sons. Ram was born to Kaushalya, the twins Lakshman and Shatrughana to Sumitra and Bharat to Kaikeyi.

In another part of the palace Queen Sunaina was very nervous yet excited as she supervised the arrangements for the Sage's visit. A room had to be prepared for the Rishi should he want to rest, although Rishi Narada never stayed in one place for more than a couple of hours. Meanwhile the staff in the kitchen was in a state of near panic trying to recall what they had cooked the last time the Rishi was at the palace. The Rishi had loved the fare and had said he would return, to experience the feast again. Each one remembered a different item on the menu and by the end of the discussion the list was so long that it would seem vulgar to serve even half the dishes in that time of famine. Sunaina and the Chief Cook then brought down the list to a critical number making sure that dishes of all the six tastes – sweet, sour, salty, bitter, chilly and astringent were included and the spread would be in keeping with the status of Janak and the famine in the kingdom. Sunaina recounted

---

[6]   Ritual offerings accompanied by the chanting of Vedic Mantras to Fire to propitiate the Gods

later that she was at a loss to understand her nervousness and excitement at the Dev-Rishi's appearance since this was not his first visit, later events would reveal the reason. Rishi Narada, King Janak, Rishi Satananda the chief court priest and Kushadhwaj the younger brother of the king then sat down to lunch served by Sunaina and the court ladies. After a sumptuous meal during which the Rishi engaged the audience with tales from the Puranas, Rishi Narada blessed Sunaina with peace, prosperity and contentment, raising his hand in blessing the Sage disappeared into another loka.

Paying heed to Rishi Narada's advice Rishi Sringi was invited to conduct a Yagna to propitiate the Goddess of the Earth or Bhudevi. Offerings of food grains, sesame seeds and ghee were made to the sacred fire accompanied by the chanting of mantras by 108 rhitwiks[7]. Then using a brand new plough yoked to which were two white bulls King Janak began the ritual ploughing of the fields. A short distance into the field, the plough struck something in the earth. The obstruction was a casket and in that lay an infant girl. Janak gently lifted her and tears welled in his eyes as he held the baby close; when he handed her to the Queen he is reported to have asked her to hold Janaki or the daughter of Janak. Rishi Satananda the Chief Priest blessed the baby with the words "Take happiness wherever you go". It was a Tuesday; the ninth day of the bright fortnight or Shukla Paksha of Vaishakha[8], and the star was the 'Pushya

---

[7]   Rhitwiks are priests who accompany the main priest during a yagna; 108 is sacred number according to Hindu Philosophy.

[8]   Corresponding to April-May of the Georgian Calendar

Nakshatra' or the Delta Cancri Constellation. It was then that Janak and Sunaina understood the significance of Rishi Narada's blessings. Thus I began my journey on this earth. What a coincidence this was, since my husband was also born on the ninth day of the bright fortnight, but in the month of Chaitra[9].

I was told that on the sixth day of my appearance on the earth the King officially announced the birth of a child, with ritual offering to the fire. Sweets, gifts, gold coins and cows were distributed to the priests. My father gave my mother a seven strand gold and coral necklace, with a caveat that it was to be given to Janaki on her wedding day. My ladies-in-waiting would never tire of describing events of my infancy. The naming ceremony was conducted on the twelfth day, early in the evening. It was a Saturday. Rishi Satanand was the Master of Ceremonies and directed the entire function. My mother, Sunaina wore a blue and gold brocade saree and had the crib done in similar colours. The jewellery that the King and Queen presented to me, Janaki, was displayed on the posts of the crib. The naming ceremony is always a ladies' function and all the ladies of the court had been invited. Prominent among the guests were the two wives of Rishi Yajnavalkya - Katyayani and Maitreyi. At the auspicious hour, Katyayani and Maitreyi passed me around the cradle – like passing the parcel and then formally laid me in the cradle. Sunaina then leant over the cradle and whispered the name chosen by the chief priest Satananda in my infant ear; and then declared it aloud to

---

[9] Corresponding to March-April of the Georgian Calendar

the audience and Janaki was now officially, Seeta[10]. Though my father always called me Janaki, I was also known as Videhi[11], Maithili[12] and Bhudevi[13].

At the naming ceremony my ears were pierced with a golden wire. This was the first piece of jewellery I wore; I preserved them till the very end. The guests then presented their gifts. Then of course there was singing, dancing and merry making with lots to eat. Feeding others was such an important part of our lives; this was how we showed we cared for people. After this as tradition has it, Sunaina distributed sarees to the guests as they left. Mother later told me that my father had ordered the palace to be illuminated and sweets to be distributed across the Kingdom, although she was not sure if the scale of celebration was appropriate, since I was a girl and not truly the heir apparent and Videha was in a state of distress. My father thought differently; he believed I was the harbinger of good fortune, Bhudevi – one born of the earth; and he was delighted at having a child.

My meetings with Katyayani and Maitreyi which began on this day continued over the years. Rishi Yajnavalkya's hermitage was on the outskirts of Mithila, and I never missed an opportunity to accompany my father to the Sage's home. In later years I was allowed to go on my own in a palanquin accompanied by my lady-in-waiting. As a child I just played around in the courtyard with the deer and

---

[10] The line made by the plough or "furrow"
[11] Belonging to Videha
[12] One from Mithila
[13] Goddess of the Earth

fed the birds, later I would pose them questions about life, questions that I hesitated to ask anybody in the palace.

As I had arrived without any notice I am told there was panic in the palace. A wet nurse was identified; she was a robust lady of a pleasant disposition who had just given birth to a son and what an honour it was to be wet nurse to the princess! My ladies-in-waiting appointed at this time stayed with me till the very end. The palace suddenly blossomed into 'song' with everybody humming their favourite rhymes and lullabies.

Since my mother was not in confinement and did not have to recoup, she spent her energies on the wet nurse, feeding her well, ensuring she had adequate rest and making sure she was always in a good mood. When I was not at her breast I was in mother's lap; this physical closeness gives babies great emotional security which expresses itself in adulthood. My mother had to make sure that she, the baby and the room were presentable at all times since Father walked in ever so often to admire his little baby. My ladies-in-waiting told me I was pink, with a mop of curly black hair and lots of hair on my little body. The nurse maids had already begun discussion on what powders they would use to rid me of my body-hair – although I had not even cut my first tooth!

Every mile stone in my first year, like opening and closing my fists; lifting my head; attempts to roll over, called for a celebration and special sweets. Since I was a girl, other ceremonies were conducted in the odd months. At seven months my '*Annaprasana*' or first solid food eating ceremony was held. My first solid food was rice powder cooked in sweetened milk. It remained one of my favourite foods, but whole grains of rice replaced rice powder which were cooked in sweetened milk, sprinkled liberally with almonds and raisins and flavoured with green cardamom. I am told I started crawling at six months; my first coherent words were 'Ma' and took my first steps shortly after I was a year old. What an achievement for a little one, and when applauded by adults confidence and self esteem was reinforced step by step. The celebration of mile stones an expression of joy of the adults, was encouragement for me, the child to move ahead.

I was told that I was good and a happy baby and rarely cried, although I would keep the nurse up all night and slept only at the crack of dawn, and all this in a happy mood; there was no 'cure' for this ailment, it lasted about six months and then just disappeared one day. I was however prone to attacks of colic and my heart rending cries kept everybody up, I screamed even louder if anybody other than my parents carried me. No crooning, no patting, no amount of aniseed water would soothe me, my parents would take turns to carry me and just walk around with me, till the pain eased. My father would say that a child with colic pain could make even the mightiest warrior dejected at his inadequacy and helplessness in dealing with the situation!

As the months passed I began to be decked with jewellery; first came the earrings at twelve days, a few weeks later a chain with a locket to ward off evil. Golden bracelets with black beads followed as did golden anklets with bells. Convention dictates that only royalty wear anklets and toe rings of gold; all others wear silver anklets and toe rings. After my first birthday without any ceremony my head was shaved bald. That was the first and last time a pair of scissors touched my hair, we were told that if scissors so much as touched a girl's hair, she would get bald overnight and remain so for the rest of her life, and then of course nobody would marry her! We swallowed this hook, line and sinker; the prospect of being bald for the rest of our lives was too terrifying for us to even contemplate testing out the belief, so it was, - for generations before us and for generations after us.

An evening ritual that I can remember forever and till the evening before my wedding was the 'warding off the evil eye' ritual. One of the maids-in-waiting would arrive with red chillies and salt in her fists just as the evening lamps were being lit. She would draw circles counter clock wise in the air around me, reciting 'mantras' and then rush out and throw the chillies and salt on a burning cow dung cake at the far corner of the court yard.

The year I appeared on this earth there was plenty of rain in Videha, the farmers had sown paddy - the life blood of Videha and the Rain God nourished their fields. Every home was happy and looked forward to the festivals of the month of Shravan[14], which is the holiest month of the Hindu calendar. The festival 'Teej' heralds the arrival of the month of Shravan. 'Teej' is the celebration of the reunion of Parvati and Shiva after hundreds of years. This is followed

---

[14] Corresponding to July-August of the Georgian Calendar

by Nag[15] Panchami[16], a day to pray to the sacred cobra to protect the people. Mondays of the month are dedicated to Shiva; it was during this month that the Churning of the Ocean took place and Lord Shiva drank poison to save the world. Shiva held the poison in his throat which is why his neck turned blue and so another name for Shiva is NeelKanth or blue-throated. Rishi Narada's blessing and the fruit of the yagna were being manifested.

My mother's name, Sunaina, meant "one with beautiful eyes" and she did have the loveliest brown eyes. Mother was fair and petite; she barely reached my father's shoulder. Her thick brown curly hair reached her knees and she styled it in a different bun everyday. She always wore flowers in her hair; her lady-in-waiting told me that when my father first saw mother she had worn flowers in her hair and he had loved it. So the flowers were worn to please her husband! Her delicate wrists were always adorned with bangles made of gold, some studded with precious stones like rubies, sapphires or pearls. She wore a rather ornate nose pin everyday, and on special occasions she wore a heavy nose ring held up with a chain that was pinned to the side of her head.

My father was the opposite of my mother in every way - he was tall and had broad shoulders, he was dark brown and had dark eyes and jet black hair. He sported a beard and tended his hair and beard with great care. Father was very

---

[15] Snake
[16] Fifth day of the fortnight

26

particular about his appearance, almost vain. As King, his people would emulate him and he had to set the standard.

When I was about eight months old, my mother discovered that the Rishi's blessings had not manifested completely, and now she was pregnant. My sister Urmila arrived a couple of months later. I was too little to recall her birth and her early years. I was told she was a serious child and smiled only when there was something to really smile about. She was darker than I, and had my mother's features and father's straight black hair. She left my mother's shoulder only when father picked her up. She yelled every time her nanny picked her up; this carried on till she was about a year old; after that Nanny and Urmila were inseparable, till Nanny left the earth. The rites of passage, announcing the birth of a child and naming were conducted for Urmila as well, but on a smaller scale. Mother said Urmila started speaking very early and by the time she was a year old she was speaking complete sentences.

A couple of months before Urmila was born, my uncle Kushadhwaj's Queen, Ganga, bore a daughter, Mandavi and a couple of years later another daughter, Shrutakirti. About the time I was seven years old, King Sudhanva the ruler of Sankasya[17] made a claim to the bow of Shiva that was in my father's custody; a fierce battle ensued and Sudhanva was defeated. Thereupon my uncle Kushadhwaj was anointed the king of Sankasya, and Mandavi and Shrutakirti moved

---

[17]   In present day Farrukhabad District of Uttar Pradesh India, 45 Kms north of Kannauj

to Sankasya with their parents. However, the four of us got together three or four times in the year- either Mandavi and Shrutakirti came visiting or Urmila and I went to Sankasya.

As we grew older I was the quieter one and Urmila lived up to her name – Urmila, meaning "one who enchants". The enchantress would be the centre of attraction in any gathering. Urmila narrated a simple incident with so many embellishments that it always became an uproarious narration with the audience in splits of laughter. She had the gift of seeing the funny side of every event – except once, and that is the only time I saw my little sister weep.

CHAPTER 2
Growing Years

The parakeets or the conch bearers, I never could tell who heralded the day, but it was after the conch was blown that one heard the bards singing praises of the ruling dynasty and the King; and the entire palace was awake. There was teeming activity in every corner of the palace, the first lamps were lit in the kitchen as 'kumkum' and 'turmeric powder' were offered to Agni, the God of Fire and 'Annapurna' the Goddess of food and nourishment; then the kitchen fires lit. There were two kitchens in the royal living quarters. One of the kitchens was strictly vegetarian where even onions and garlic were taboo. The cooks belonged to the Brahmin caste and other than the cooks no one, including us, could enter the kitchen. The food was placed on a platform outside the kitchen and was taken to the dining hall by the bearers. Offerings to the Gods were also cooked here. As we belonged to the warrior class, or the Kshatriya caste, the family ate a non-vegetarian diet except on certain days. Non-vegetarian food was cooked in the second kitchen; the cooks here belonged to the Kshatriya caste. Rules about entering this kitchen were not as strict as in the first kitchen; we could enter the kitchen but only bare foot and after the chief cook sprinkled water over the visitor – a ritual cleansing; however one could not enter any kitchen without completing the morning ablutions and a bath. The cooks in the vegetarian kitchen got busy first, huge jugs of cows' milk that had arrived as soon as the cows were milked, had to be heated and then curds set for the day and morning tea brewed for everyone. Then the cooks got busy preparing breakfast.

Apart from the family and guests, over a hundred people ate at the palace at every meal. There were kitchens for the in-house staff and the outer house staff. The in-house staff were the maids-in-waiting and some of the courtiers. The outer house staff included the guards, the charioteers and the gardeners. The Ministers, other high ranking officials and the ladies-in-waiting ate from our kitchen. There was a strict hierarchy with regard to meal times. Strictly at the appointed hour food was offered at the temple of Shiva and Parvati and only then served to us. However, the food was not served unless the King, (or when he was away the Queen), sat down for a meal. Once the family finished their meal, surplus food from the royal table was served to the in-house staff along with the food that was cooked for them; after the in-house staff had finished eating the outer-house staff was served. At noon, food was distributed to the poor, at the palace gate.

My parents rose early, they began their day with a visit to the family temple. The family temple was within the palace grounds - here Shiva and his consort Parvati were the main deities but Lord Ganesh without whom no temple is complete, occupied an important place in the temple. I knew that my parents were at the temple when the temple bells began to peal. Shiva the greatest of them all, is easily appeased, cold water poured over the Shivling is said to please him the most. So my father would pour water over the Shivling, accompanied by the chanting of the Rudram – a Hindu hymn dedicated to Lord Shiva, as he prayed for the welfare of Videha. After this ritual my father would take a long walk into the city, and return to the palace for the morning meal. Meanwhile my mother would be in her personal altar in the palace - her personal deity was Vishnu. Vishnu, it is believed, loves adornment. So, my mother would adorn the deity in a fresh set of clothes and ornaments everyday. Some days the ornaments were of gold studded with precious stones, on other days my mother would create armlets and necklaces with strings of flowers. There was a small kitchenette in her palace where she herself cooked her offerings to Vishnu and then shared it with us during breakfast. Her offering to Vishnu tasted 'divine'. Vishnu loves white butter and so she would offer him freshly churned white butter and rice cooked in milk and sugar, or roasted flattened rice with jaggery. Whatever the offering, it was always sweet and flavoured with cardamom. Mother's engagement with her Lord was elaborate and took the same time that my father took to walk around the city.

Our maids-in-waiting would be urging us to get out of bed and get ready in time for breakfast. Both Urmila and I would hear the conches and the pealing of the temple bells but would pretend to be asleep, particularly in the winter months. Some days I would be awake even before the birds began to twitter, but it was so comfortable to just lie in bed. Once we had been brought out from under the covers, Urmila and I spent enormous time making up our minds about what to wear. We wore ankle length skirts – called 'lehenga' and short blouses or cholis, and as we grew up we graduated to carrying an 'odhini' – a length of unstitched cloth tucked in at the waist on the left going around the back and the loose end taken over the left shoulder covering the chest; and then on to sarees. Once the lehenga, choli and odhini were identified came the turn of the jewellery; looking back, I was full of admiration for the patience of the maids. Then came the massage with warm mustard oil in the winter and coconut oil in the summer followed by a bath with exfoliating packs made of herbs; after our baths we anointed ourselves with either jasmine, sandalwood or rose perfumed oils. Finally we were ready to appear in public.

If after all this, I had time before breakfast, I rushed to the Shiva Parvati temple. Parvati was my role model, father had told me how Parvati had fasted for long years to marry Shiva and finally she was married to him. I vowed to be a wife like Parvati and secretly waited for the day my Shiva could come and take me to his home. When we were young, marriage was the 'ultimate' milestone of our lives. Marriage and wedding were synonymous to us. I realised later it was around the 'wedding' that we had built our dreams. Marriage I discovered was a long journey with a partner across soft grass and over hard stones and once that journey began there was no going back alone or together one just moved on ahead.

In the large dining hall we greeted our parents, prostrating at their feet; not once did I look at them and not think to myself what a handsome couple they made! My mother was always perfectly dressed. She wore a different colour saree everyday honouring the nine planets, on Sunday she wore red or orange the colour of the king of planets the Sun; on Mondays for the queen of planets the moon she wore white or silver; on Tuesdays the day of Mars she wore pinks and reds; on Wednesdays she honoured Mercury the prince of planets with various shades of Green; Golden yellow was reserved for Jupiter on Thursdays, Venus was honoured on Friday with various shades of white, Saturday is the day of Saturn, Dragon's head and the Dragon's tail, so it was black or blue. Her jewellery, crafted by the best jewellers in the kingdom, always complemented her sarees. She was particular about highlighting her big eyes with kohl that she made herself. One knew she was around when the scent of jasmine perfume wafted in, no matter what the season or the occasion she always smelt of jasmine. I think my father liked that fragrance, when I asked her once why she always used jasmine; she coyly turned away and changed the subject.

My parents never publicly displayed their love for each other; in the presence of their children, the subject of their conversations was, children, food, the garden and perhaps some matters of the state. Despite that, their love, respect and concern for each other was apparent. They followed a set code of conduct, neither raised their voice at each other; if they disagreed, my father would raise one eyebrow, every so slightly, that only my mother and in later year we sisters saw. No sooner did my father indicate the slightest displeasure,

Mother rushed off to get him some sweets. If my mother was upset she pursed her lips which only my father saw, and only when he pointed it out to us, we realised something had disturbed her; if she was extremely upset she would ask my father to allow her to visit her parents. When that request came my father would agree immediately, "Of course you may go", he would say, "but take me with you, I'll die without you", and that would end the dispute!

My father sat down to breakfast in the large dining hall, he sat on a cushion on the floor and ate off silverware placed on a low stool. The Prime Minister would be in attendance briefing him on state matters. We ladies stood in the background and as soon as father was served and serious discussions began we withdrew to the inner dining hall, where we ladies had our breakfast over much chatter and giggling.

After breakfast it was school time, we were twelve of us in the class. Urmila, myself and ten other girls who were the daughters of Ministers in the court. Our teacher was a middle aged man, with a hot temper; he told us stories from the Puranas each with a moral and taught us the correct intonations while chanting mantras. Everyday we would have to narrate a story that the teacher had earlier told us, in this way stories have been passed down generations. Consider this, if one mother did not know a story an entire generation and generations to come would never hear the story. If any of us forgot a detail in the story or forgot a mantra, his eyes blazed fire, we were terrified of him. But as we grew up and he grew old we just loved him and went across to his home to listen to even more stories and eat the sweetmeats his wife offered us.

The next class was logic and maths. We had to solve puzzles and problems. We were also taught multiplication tables, tables of 1/2, 1/4, 1/8, and 1/16 for example ½ x 2=1 and so on. Although we would never need to engage in calculation, memorising was considered the best way of sharpening the intellect. It was in the logic class that we were taught to play chess, I loved the game and would often play with the teacher, my father and later with my husband, and I was most often able to checkmate my husband.

After our morning school was over we had lunch and were allowed a siesta, we were twelve giggling girls and so there was no question of a siesta. It was during the afternoons that we played hide and seek in the palace corridors; another favourite was a ball game. The game required one ball less than the number of players, one of us would roll all the balls down the corridors and the others ran to retrieve them, whoever did not retrieve a ball had to do a forfeit; and the player who had retrieved the maximum number of balls could roll them in the next round. We would play this game for hours on end. One afternoon I was rather unlucky and could not retrieve a ball even once. Just then I saw a ball roll under a long wooden box at the end of the corridor, and Ujwala one of the girls charged towards it, but could not retrieve the ball from under the box, and she gave up the ball as lost. I dragged my feet towards the box, the day had been unlucky and if Ujwala who was taller and stronger than me couldn't lift the box, how could I? I bent down and surprisingly lifted the box with my left hand and retrieved the ball. My father happened to be passing by, he stopped, "Janaki! What did you just do?" he asked; I was perplexed I just held out the ball. "Where was the ball?" was the next question, I pointed to the place under the box. "How did you reach it?" his voice was urgent. I was thoroughly puzzled by now; why was my father behaving so strange, I had only retrieved a ball from under the box; without saying a word I just lifted the box again. I can never forget the expression on my father's face, - there was amazement and joy. He held me close, kissed me on the forehead and exclaimed, "I always thought you were special; today I am convinced"; I didn't understand what he meant, but I was too confused to figure it out, I let it pass and we returned to our game.

Father then told me that the box contained the bow of Shiva which had been given to the Janaks for safe keeping by Sage Parshuram, while he did penance in the forests. It was this very bow over which my father went to war with Sudhanva the King of Sankasya and defeated him. My father told me that the bow was very heavy and an ordinary mortal could not even move the bow leave alone lift it; only one with divine powers could have lifted it, and the man who lifted the bow would be the one I would marry. The latter part of the story made little sense to this eight year old. The only part I understood was since I had lifted the bow, I would marry the man who could also lift the bow. I hoped my husband would be as good looking as my father; I always wanted my husband to be dark; fair men I thought were very effeminate. My father was dark and mother fair and so I believed that was how all couples should be.

36

My mother would receive guests in the afternoon or would attend a ladies' get together. Ladies get togethers were functions to celebrate someone's pregnancy, a naming ceremony or a baby's first solid food eating ceremony. There was one function at the end of the first trimester of pregnancy and another one after the seventh month of pregnancy. Urmila and I loved attending these functions because when we said our goodbyes we always received gifts. When ladies came visiting, my mother insisted we greet the visitors and then we were free to go out and play in the palace gardens. But, when Rishi Satananda's wife came visiting I would stay on, she was a storehouse of information about plants and medicinal herbs, the significance of various fasts and she had an interesting style of narration. I learnt a great many new words just listening to her and used them when I had to narrate a story in class; needless to say the teacher was most often pleased with my narration. Later in life I would thank the unseen power that motivated me to stay on and learn about plants and herbs. Our growing years were fun filled and we were secure, much loved and cherished.

Although we were princesses my mother was particular that we had a direct experience of house keeping, so that when we were married off, our in-laws would not have an occasion to find fault with the princesses of Videha. On the days that we did not have study classes, she insisted that we help the maids-in-waiting do our rooms and spend time in the kitchens. The cooks would ask us to help them – we were given a handful of peas to shell or a fistful of rice to pick and then they would tell whoever would listen that Urmila and Seeta helped get the meal ready. Mother would get us to cook in her kitchen, her cooking philosophy was to cook with minimum fuss, minimum spices and conserve energy - for example she cooked peas with only salt and a green chilly and would take the pan off the fire just before the peas were done. "They'll be done in the warmth of their own heat now", she would say. In later years when I had to cook with minimum support, I relived these times in mother's kitchenette.

Through the year there were many festivals, feasts and fasts. The beginning of summer and the beginning of winter are two very important junctions of climatic and solar influence. The year would begin with the 'Vasant Navaratri'[18] in the month of Chaitra which heralds the beginning of summer; in the month of Ashwin[19] which heralds the winter was the second Navaratri or the 'Sharad Navaratri'. For nine days the source of energy the Divine Mother or Shakti was worshipped in her various forms. The Sharad Navaratri would culminate in Dussehera or the day on which the Durga aspect of the Divine Mother killed the demon Mahishasur. Mahishasur represents the demons of ego, anger, jealousy and the like that dwell in our mind. This was a period when we followed a restricted diet which apart from being a spiritual exercise served to acclimatise the body to the change of season and of food. During the first four days we reduced our diet progressively, on the fifth day we ate only fruit; thereafter we gradually increased our diet, to

---

[18] Nav-nine; Ratri-Nights
[19] Corresponding to September-October of the Georgian Calendar

begin eating the fruits and vegetables that belonged to the coming season.

After the scorching summer came the month of Shravan, the month of rain, the more the rainfall the greater was the enthusiasm to celebrate the many festivals of Shravan. Urmila loved the festival of Teej, she loved wearing glass bangles and on Teej she could have as many as she wanted. The bangle seller would come to sell bangles to the ladies in the palace and Urmila would be there every time he came, even normally Urmila would be wearing at least a dozen bangles, but during the month of Shravan she wore bangles from elbows to wrists. My father would tease her endlessly, he would say she sounded like the milkman's wife with her jangling bangles, but Urmila wouldn't be affected – she had her bangles.

Diwali the most important of all festivals was celebrated, on the new moon night of the month of Kartik[20]. At this time the Sun is in the Libra constellation, and is at its weakest in terms of spiritual power and hence the evil forces are at their height. This is why this new moon night is considered the darkest night of the year. To counter the evil forces Lakshmi the Goddess of wealth and prosperity comes down to the earth to bless her devotees. Homes were lit up with oil lamps to welcome the Goddess; beyond attaining material wealth the spiritual significance of Diwali is associated with the lights dispelling darkness within us with the light of subtle

---

[20] Corresponding to October-November of the Georgian Calendar

knowledge and overcoming evil with good. Preparations for the festival began days in advance, with homes being cleaned; sweets being prepared and everybody getting a new set of clothes, all to welcome the Goddess Lakshmi.

Through the years, we girls fasted on Thursdays; it was believed that young girls who fasted on Thursdays got a good husband. We had a special diet that day, and we eagerly waited for our meals! In the evening we got dressed in our finery and went to the Shiva Parvati temple at the edge of the town. At the temple we met other girls and would spend time chatting away and playing in the gardens around the temple. When Mandavi and Shrutakirti came to Mithila they too would accompany us. The fasting was for a good husband so invariably the topic would turn to marriage. As I was the eldest among the girls I was first in line. We usually discussed what kind of a husband we wanted, Mandavi and I were certain we wanted a tall, dark and handsome husband. Urmila and Shrutakirti were clear they would not marry a dark man. One time we discussed what kind of wives we would like to be. Parvati was my role model so I said, "My husband will be my world and I will never be away from him". Urmila said, "I am quite used to listening to whatever you, Seeta, say so I will accept my husband's wishes". Mandavi was pensive, "I think I will do whatever my husband wants me to do", she said. Shrutakirti the youngest of all said, "What kind of a wife do I want to be? What kind of a question is that? I will be a loving wife, that's all!"

As if on another plane, father would be in court conducting state business, travelling to other towns but whenever he had a chance he would organise philosophical debates. After the incident of my lifting the wooden box, my father asked me to come and sit with him as the debate was in progress. I didn't understand anything for a long time, but I liked being there. When Gargi, the daughter of Rishi Vachaknu, got up to speak I couldn't take my eyes off her, she was so eloquent, so graceful and yet so powerful. Once she even took on Rishi Yaagnavalkya himself, the Rishi had silenced many a speaker in the past, but at one point, even he was at a loss to answer Gargi. Sometimes my father would lean over and explain a thought expressed, other times he would ask for my opinion. On one occasion father repeated what I said to Rishi Yaagnavalkya, and the Rishi looked towards me and nodded in appreciation. My confidence in myself soared and after that I took even keener interest in attending the debates.

Rishi Yaagnavalkya lived on the outskirts of Mithila; he had two wives, Maitreyi and Katyayani. Polygamy was common in society although my father took only one wife, whom he loved dearly and she was his best friend. My father would visit the Sage often and I would often accompany my father. The Rishi's wives were happy to see me and would take me around the ashram gardens. Vegetables for the Rishi, his family and the students were grown in the ashram, I learnt a lot from them about growing vegetables, selecting the right ones to cook and the right ones to pick to store. On occasion I helped them hoe the ground and even plant a few saplings. I visited the hermitage so often, even the cows recognised me and then Maitreyi taught me how to milk a cow. In the palace I would never have been permitted to hoe the vegetable beds or milk a cow. I would ask Maitreyi questions about creation and the creator as we milked the cows or hoed the vegetable beds; Maitreyi always answered my questions in a way that I understood. I was closer to Maitreyi than I was to Katyayani although I loved them equally. As I grew up I was troubled by nightmares, a recurring nightmare was that I was alone among strange looking people. I would get up wet with perspiration and couldn't go back to sleep. I shared my fear with Maitreyi who enveloped me in her arms, sat me in her lap and assured me that in every situation God would be with me and that I had nothing to fear.

After attending a couple of debates where I heard Gargi I hesitantly asked her if I could come to her home, she was more than welcoming. She lived a little distance from Mithila and so I would spend a couple of days with her every time I visited her. Gargi gave me undivided attention; she was a yogi, and initiated me into various techniques of yoga.

As I approached my teens, kings from various kingdoms came to my father with a proposal of marriage. Who would not want an alliance with Janak and what better way than to marry his daughter? Janaki was incidental; it was Janak's daughter that mattered. My father would then take them to the wooden box at the end of the corridor and tell them the condition on which the alliance with his daughter rested; that was the last of that attempted alliance! Rishi Satananda then decided that it was time for a public 'Swayamwar'[21].

---

[21]   Practice in Ancient India of a girl choosing her suitor. The

Messengers were sent out announcing the Swayamwar and the condition attached to winning the bride. In Mithila arrangements were in full swing, a huge pavilion was built for the competition, palaces built for the many kings who were expected and guesthouses constructed to house the many guests. There was excitement everywhere as my trousseau was readied. My ladies-in-waiting and the maids who would accompany me were equally excited as they got ready to depart with me to my husband's home.

Once the Swayamwar had been announced I detected a change in my father; when he returned from the court in the evening, he would send for both of us, "Janaki and Urmila come sit and talk to me". Urmila as the baby of the house was rather impatient and after a few minutes she would run off. My father would then tell me what he expected of me as the future daughter-in-law of a great kingdom. "Take happiness wherever you go; your duty towards your husband is of paramount importance; your sons should be brought up to inherit the throne not by their birth alone but by their ability, so bring them up well; bring up your daughters to be jewels in the crown of another's home". "Father, how are you so sure I will marry into a great family?" I ventured once, when I had heard these musings for the nth time. "Janaki, only the scion of a particular lineage will be able to lift the bow" he smiled, his gentle smile. But my heart skipped a beat, did I see right? My father's beard was speckled with white, how come I did not notice it before? Was my father

---

Sanskrit word 'Swayam' meaning self; and Var meaning husband

growing old? My face must have reflected sadness because my father said, "What ails thee little one? Rest assured your husband will be the best of all men, and you will never be far from me". I shook myself out of the mood and went and hugged him, feeling his prickly beard on my cheek as I nestled into a warm comforting embrace.

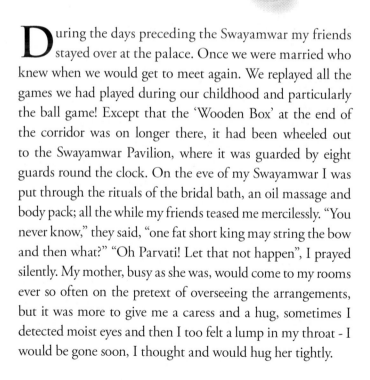

CHAPTER 3
The Swayamwar

During the days preceding the Swayamwar my friends stayed over at the palace. Once we were married who knew when we would get to meet again. We replayed all the games we had played during our childhood and particularly the ball game! Except that the 'Wooden Box' at the end of the corridor was on longer there, it had been wheeled out to the Swayamwar Pavilion, where it was guarded by eight guards round the clock. On the eve of my Swayamwar I was put through the rituals of the bridal bath, an oil massage and body pack; all the while my friends teased me mercilessly. "You never know," they said, "one fat short king may string the bow and then what?" "Oh Parvati! Let that not happen", I prayed silently. My mother, busy as she was, would come to my rooms ever so often on the pretext of overseeing the arrangements, but it was more to give me a caress and a hug, sometimes I detected moist eyes and then I too felt a lump in my throat - I would be gone soon, I thought and would hug her tightly.

The morning of the day before the Swayamwar was a busy one; my mother had invited the wives of Ministers, Courtiers and her friends for a ceremony to bless me. Five married ladies anointed me with turmeric paste and kumkum, blessing me with a husband who was best among all men. Sage Yaagnavalkya's wives Katyayani and Maitreyi came laden with flowers and fruits from their garden. They had to travel quite a distance to reach the palace and so I didn't quite expect them to come - I was overjoyed on seeing them. Maitreyi also brought with her, fresh milk from my favourite cow. The two hugged me tight and blessed me with peace and joy; Maitreyi had tears in her eyes and that moved me to weep copiously, but with the singing and dancing in the background I was soon distracted and joined in the merry- making.

After the women had left I had a surprise visitor, the Sage Gargi. As a renunciate, she would not participate in these social functions and so chose a time when the family would be on their own. I felt so honoured that a Sage of her stature should make the time and effort to come to the palace to meet me. I prostrated at her feet, and she lifted me and held me close. She then held me at arm's length and looked into my eyes; it was as if she was passing a message. Placing her hand on my head in blessing she said, "Maithili, I have passed on to you all the knowledge I possess, it will come to you at the appropriate time. Continue with your yoga practices and all will be well". At that point in time we all thought she had blessed me with a good husband and a good family to marry into or with sons; so important for a queen to establish her position in the court. Much later I would realise how priceless her teachings and blessings were.

After lunch Urmila and I were summoned to my father's chambers. Rishi Satananda, his wife, my parents and my uncle Kushadhwaj Janak, the King of Sankasya, and his wife Ganga, were discussing the Swayamwar. The Rishi and his wife gave my parents, Urmila and me instructions on how we were to conduct ourselves the next day. Just then a messenger arrived with a note for the Rishi; it must have been an important matter for a messenger to interrupt such a private meeting. Indeed it was, the Rishi Vishwamitra along with two princes had arrived on the outskirts of Mithila. My father along with Rishi Satananda and the courtiers, made haste to receive the great Sage ; it was a great honour to the house of Janak for Rishi Vishwamitra to arrive in Mithila.

Later that afternoon, my dearest friend Uttara, who knew everything about everybody, came into the palace bubbling with gossip about the two princes with Sage Vishwamitra. "They are the sons of Dashrath, the King of Ayodhya; they have come with their Guru, Rishi Vishwamitra. Unlike the other princes they do not have chariots or servants with them, they have come on foot from the Rishi's hermitage in the forest and not from their Kingdom. One of them is dark and tall; the other is slightly shorter and fair. The dark one is Ram and the fair one is Lakshman". "Fair and sweet, that's the one for you Urmila", we all teased. We were all eager for more and Uttara was bursting to tell. "I heard on the way to the palace, that both the brothers are great warriors and they have killed many demons. But do you know I heard the dark prince has magic feet, on his way here he touched a stone and a woman sprang out of the stone".

"I am told they are here for the Swayamwar", said Uttara. "I heard the princes took a walk around the city, they are so good looking and have such majestic personalities that the entire population followed them around". Urmila snapped, "I heard and I am told is all what you have been saying, what did you see for yourself?" Uttara sighed, "If I had seen would I be here? Let's go out for a drive, may be we will see them."

A visit to the Shiva Parvati temple at the edge of the town every evening had become a ritual. About ten giggling girls would reach the temple in the early evening. We first bowed to Lord Ganesh, the remover of all obstacles and I would silently call to Ganesh "Oh Ganesha! Let there be no obstacles in the way of the Swayamwar; look I've brought pieces of sugar cane which you love". After paying obeisance to Shiva and Parvati we would wander around the temple precincts. The gardeners would help us pick flowers which we strung into garlands to offer the deities before the evening prayer. At the appointed hour the temple bells would peal and the dark sanctum sanctorum would be bright as day with hundreds of oil lamps lit all around and the chanting of the prayers would begin. The precious stones studded in the jewellery on the deities reflected the light from the lamps and glowed. I loved the way the diamond in the nose ring of Goddess Parvati, would wink at me, and emit a blue light. The diamond, I was told, was gifted to my great grandfather by a king who ruled in the South of India, beyond the River Narmada. It was such a precious and rare gem that it was appropriate it should adorn the Goddess and not a mere mortal, never mind if she was a queen. As I stood in front of Shiva and Parvati with my hands folded in supplication I would pray, 'Oh Goddess Parvati, I promise to be a wife like you, let my husband be the best among all men".

Normally we would be chattering on our way to the temple, but that day there was silence as we peered through the curtained windows of our palanquins in the hope of seeing these fabled princes; disappointed, we alighted at the temple gates. I rushed to my Ganesh and offered him the sugar cane I had brought for him. We spent a good hour after that, collecting flowers and stringing them into garlands. Just as we got up to enter the sanctum for the evening prayer, Uttara and Swati came rushing in, their eyes sparkling in delight. There! There! They pointed to a spot beyond the frangipani tree. "What and where?" we asked, "The princes!" they gasped, "are plucking flowers". I was at the tail end of the group and when we turned around I was ahead of everybody. At first I did not see anybody and so I moved out further into the temple courtyard, the tinkling of the bells on my anklets must have caught the attention of princes and one of them turned around. Just then I caught sight of him, and he saw me too! Oh my God! First something burst in my head, then in my ears and my heart was pounding. I had never seen anybody like him, he was very tall, taller than my father, and very dark. His eyes were black and large and he had black curly hair; I was riveted to the spot, and we just stared at each other. I am sure everybody must have heard my heart pounding; after what seemed an eternity, my friends started giggling and the reverie was broken. We both turned away at the same instant, I was so embarrassed, my cheeks hot, my ears were burning and my heart wouldn't stop pounding. I could never recall walking back to the altar for the evening prayer, I prayed ferverently to Parvati, "Please Mother let it be him who lifts the bow, he is so slender, but please give him strength to lift the bow". When I bowed my head at the feet of the Mother, a garland offered to her fell on my bowed head. This was an indication! The Mother had answered my prayer. He would lift the bow!

On our return to the palace my friends teased me mercilessly, "You wanted a dark husband, and your desire is fulfilled. Surely he will string the bow". I wished I could have disappeared into the earth - I was so embarrassed at having made a fool of myself. I wanted silence to relive those magical moments, but there was no let up from the teasing.

After dinner Urmila came skipping in to relate what she had overheard my father tell my mother. "I had not sent an invitation to King Dashrath, of the Ikshavakus of Kosala, as I was told his sons were in some hermitage. But today I met the sons of King Dashrath; their names are Ram and Lakshman. Rishi Vishwamitra had taken the boys to his hermitage and has brought them here. Rishi Vishwamitra told me about their achievements, imagine Ram killed Tadaka the demoness with a single arrow and trying to kill her so many kings have lost their lives. There is more! On the way to Mithila, the three passed by Rishi Gautam's ashram. Some sand particles on which Ram had walked flew and landed on a stone statue and lo and behold! A lady trapped in the statue was set free from a curse. She clasped Ram's feet and wept - her tears of gratitude wet the ground around Ram's feet. She was Ahalya who had been cursed by her husband Rishi Gautam".

"Ahalya was renowned for her beauty; the God Indra coveted her and was determined to have her. When Indra could no longer bear the pangs of desire, he decided to act. Indra knew that Rishi Gautam would go to the river for his morning ablutions when the cock crowed, and so one morning he mimicked the crowing of the cock earlier than usual and when Rishi Gautam was safely out of sight Indra arrived at Ahalya's doorstep disguised as Rishi Gautam. Ahalya was not deceived but her pride in her beauty and the thought of a God coming to woo her blinded her judgment and the two spent some time together. They were shaken out of their paradise when they heard the footsteps of the Rishi. There was no time for a cover up; in any case the Rishi could see beyond, and while Indra fled, Gautam cursed Ahalya to become a stone and lie unnoticed till 'Ram' descended on earth, and with the dust of his feet cast off the curse".

So, the stories of the princes' greatness had an element of truth in them, I thought to myself.

My father had continued, "Ram is the one I would want as a husband for my Janaki, but he is so slender and young I wonder if he will be able to lift the bow. Perhaps the challenge of lifting the bow was rather over ambitious on my part". To which Mother had replied, "Don't worry, O King of Videha, your daughter will be married to the best of men".

This provided more ammunition to the teasers and the teasing went on late into the night and when I finally turned into bed I could only see that face. I held the garland close to me all night as I tossed and turned and slept fitfully waiting for the sun to rise. Later my husband told me that he was thunder struck and couldn't get my face out of his mind. He too was mesmerised and walked back like a zombie, his brother did not tease him but walked beside him silently and when they reached the guest house narrated the experience to Guru Vishwamitra; the Guru blessed Ram, "So be it". My husband would tell me later that as he too tossed and turned in bed that night, he saw the full moon and said to himself, "You cannot match the lustre on her face". In later years when we lived in the forest my husband would point to the full moon and say, "Look up Seeta, this is what I meant when I told the moon that he could not match the lustre on your face. Even without all your beauty baths you outshine the moon". Despite his serious exterior, my husband was very romantic.

By now the story of my being captivated by Ram was out and my maids-in-waiting had an amused expression, I could not look them in the eyes. I bathed in rose water, and was ready to be dressed. I had butterflies in my stomach and the memory of that face would not leave me. The dressing began as my feet and hands were decorated with 'Alta' a red dye which is used by ladies during religious ceremonies; the maids did my hair, strings of jasmine flowers were plaited into my hair. There was much chatter and excitement in the room as my dressing progressed, my mother came in a least half a dozen times, Urmila would rush in to see the progress and then rush back to complete her dressing. Uttara and Swati were darting in and out at various stages of their dressing, to offer suggestions. These visits were so distracting, but it was just love and excitement so nobody really wanted to tell the girls to keep off. I wore a crimson coloured silk saree with an elaborate border, embroidered in gold thread, specially woven for the occasion by a married lady. Over this I carried a stole made entirely of gold thread. In my ears were elaborate danglers of gold and pearls that reached my shoulder. Elbow to wrist my arms were covered with red and green glass bangles interspersed with bracelets made of gold, corals and pearls. My fingers were adorned with elaborate rings. My mother gifted to me the seven strand gold and coral necklace my father had given her to celebrate my birth. Once I wore that I did not need anything more to dress my neck. My gold anklets were replaced with heavier anklets, toe rings would come when I was actually married. A heavy gold band round my waist completed the ensemble. Since Urmila was not the bride she got to choose her colour and she wore her favourite green, a saree similar to mine but less elaborate; and she got to wear all the bangles she wanted. Urmila had braided her hair; her thick braid reached down to her knees. The top of the braid was decorated with a half gold cone and the end with tassels of gold. And we were ready! I went to my mother's altar and prostrated before Lord Vishnu. Then my lady-in- waiting came in with red chillies and salt to ward off all evil. When my father saw me dressed his eyes filled with tears, softly he said to my mother, because others were around, "Sunaina, put some of the kohl from your eyes on her cheek"[22]. I knew then I was looking my best.

We stepped out of the palace in a small procession, preceded by ladies holding a clay pot with a coconut encircled by

---

[22] A black dot is put on a child's face to ward off bad vibes of others, sometimes it is the kohl from the mother's eyes.

mango leaves. The thought that today would be the last time I, as Janak and Sunaina's daughter was leaving the palace, tomorrow I would enter and leave the palace as someone's wife, crossed my mind bringing a twinge of sadness. The palanquins moved slowly to allow the people to have a glimpse of me and shower flower petals. At the pavilion a special area had been created for the ladies of the palace, the ladies were always seated away from the public eye. My mother settled me, and warned Urmila, Uttara, Swati and the others that they were not to leave me alone and not to chatter. She then took her seat and closed her eyes in prayer. There were thousands of spectators all round, the prospective suitors - kings and princes from kingdoms far and near were seated in a special enclosure away from the public. In that crowd my eyes were searching for 'the dark one'; no he wasn't there, I panicked. Just then I saw the two brothers enter, walking behind their Guru, Rishi Vishwamitra. So this was the great Sage Vishwamitra! I mentally prostrated to him. I was so nervous; it was as if I had to lift the bow. My father and Rishi Satananda went up to receive them and offered them seats of honour. The 'Final Hour' had dawned, Rishi Satananda blew the conch and, the bards circled the pavilion announcing the test of trial for the suitors to win the hand of Janak's daughter. Suitor after suitor came and tried to string the bow, not one of them could even move the bow an inch leave alone string it. These were hefty warriors; although I rejoiced at each failure I began to worry how the slender dark one would lift the bow. Would my father change the conditions of the test of trial? Unlikely, I thought, then how would I marry the dark prince? When the last of these hefty warriors had tried and failed, my father rose, and in a booming voice addressed the audience, "Many of you wooed my daughter; to you I had set a simple task of stringing Shiva's bow, each one of you has failed. This means there is no warrior worth his name left on this earth. God has decreed that my daughter should remain unmarried, so be it."

At that moment there was some movement from where the Rishi Vishwamitra and the two princes were sitting. The fair one, Prince Lakshman rose, "Oh no!" I thought to myself, but Lakshman, red with anger had risen to address my father. "Oh King!" he said "Your words are inappropriate where the sons of the Raghu Dynasty are present. I can break the bow as easily as one breaks a radish and if I am unable to do so, I shall never lift a bow again. Why don't you invite us to try?" Since no invitation for the Swayamwar had been sent to King Dashrath, the Master of Ceremonies missed calling them to the dais. Ram pulled his angry younger brother back to his seat. There was a hush in the pavilion; I was delighted at this turn of events; my father, rather embarrassed at the faux pas looked in the direction of Rishi Vishwamitra, who signalled Ram to take the challenge. I stopped breathing, this was a make or break situation. The dark prince, my Ram got up, bowed to his Guru and gracefully climbed the steps up to the dais. Ram approached the bow like a lion approaching its prey, his walk was unhurried, confident and majestic. I prayed to the Lord Ganesh, "Oh Lord I have dutifully brought you sugar cane every evening, now please bless me, and lighten the weight of the bow, so that he may be able to lift it". As Ram neared the bow, our eyes met fleetingly and I shut my eyes tight. There was a resounding clap like thunder as if the heavens had broken; I covered my ears with my hands. When the reverberation had died down, there was dead silence and then there was great clapping and the musicians began playing. I slowly opened my eyes and raised my head to look at the bow, I couldn't believe what I saw, - the bow lay in two pieces! I looked up to see Ram looking straight at me, his eyes seemed to say, "You were mine from the moment I saw you". I turned my head to look around me, my mother had tears streaming down a smiling face, and father's smile reached his ears. Rishi Satananda then rose and signalled to my mother to bring me out. I was up before she could even turn around, Urmila thrust a garland made of blue lotus in my hands, then she and my friends rushed to escort me to where the dark prince, my Ram stood. I couldn't believe my luck! My hands were trembling as I garlanded him, he smiled at me, and this was the first special smile, so long only our eyes had met. I thought to myself, this is how God must look, and then looked down. I couldn't take it any more; my heart would burst with joy if I looked at him any longer. Custom dictates that the bride touch the groom's feet; when my friends urged me to do this I wouldn't, I was so scared, I thought if this magician could turn a stone into a woman why would he not turn a woman into a stone. Ram, now my husband read my mind, "Don't worry", he said, "You won't turn to stone".

Just then the great sage Rishi Parshuram made his appearance. Rishi Vishwamitra got up and greeted him and introduced him to the two princes as the sons of King Dashrath, the princes bowed to the Rishi who blessed them and then the Rishi blessed me, with a long and happy married life.

When he turned around after blessing me he caught sight of the broken bow. He roared in anger, "Janak, just what is happening here and who in the world could break this bow?" At this point I was hurriedly returned to the private enclosure. I strained my ears to hear the exchange.

My father nervously described the cause of the event, the Swayamwar, only to be silenced by the Sage, "But who broke the bow?"

I now heard Ram's voice; he spoke so sweetly, "My Lord the bow has been broken by one who would serve you. Tell me what may I do for you?"

Rishi Parshuram roared, "One who serves doesn't destroy his Master's bow and behave like an enemy would. The destroyer of the bow must stand up".

Lakshman had an amused but insolent expression on his face as he stood up and addressed the Sage, "We have destroyed so many bows in our youth, you were never angry then. Why now, what is so special about this bow?"

Rishi Parshuram turned around and I saw his fair face now purple with anger. "You fool can you not see that this is Lord Shiva's bow. Have you no fear for your life speaking to me in that tone? Have you not heard of my rage that can destroy a foetus in the womb?" Parshuram bellowed.

But Lakshman would not be silenced, "To us Kshatriyas all bows are alike, the moment Ram touched it the bow broke. It is nobody's fault, so why are you raging?" he said.

Ram, who had returned to his seat, witnessed this angry exchange without any emotion on his face. In our enclosure the ladies were trembling with fear, my mother had tears rolling down her cheeks; I was numb and transfixed to my chair as I heard this exchange.

Parshuram looked as if he would burst, "Do you know who I am? I have been a celibate since childhood and am the declared enemy of the Kshatriya Clan. I have exterminated them from this earth time and again", he shouted at Lakshman.

Still undeterred, Lakshman said, "Oh Great Master, when I saw the axe and the bow on your back I mistook you for a Kshatriya and took you on. Had I known you were you were a descendant of the Sage Bhrigu, I would not have challenged you, we Kshatriyas do not display our valour to the Gods, their devotees, Brahmins or cows. I take back every word. Nevertheless the weapons on your back do not behove the stature of a great Sage".

"Vishwamitra! Contain this young lad, he looks young but is the devil himself. Tell him about my achievements and my glory", yelled the Sage.

Rishi Vishwamitra tried to placate Parshuram asking him to forgive Lakshman, but Lakshman would not stop. He now said, "Heroes perform heroic deeds - only cowards boast of their deeds."

With this remark Lakshman had crossed the boundaries of propriety and there was murmur of displeasure from the crowd in the pavilion. I saw a severe expression on Ram's face and be beckoned Lakshman back to his seat. Lakshman returned, suitably chastised.

Ram now rose like a majestic lion. In all humility he folded his hands in front of the Sage, and in a gentle voice said, "I appeal to you My Lord; forgive the child, you know well that wasps and children are alike, they do not have the power of discrimination, and so the wise do not hold any ill will towards them. Besides, my brother is not at fault, I am the one who broke the bow. You are 'Parshuram' and I am only 'Ram'; I am your servant and at your service. Tell me what I must do to appease your anger. My head is at your feet, use your axe to sever it, do what you will, but please calm down".

Ram's placating words made no difference to the Sage, he said, "It is with your connivance that your brother taunted me and now you are giving me a sermon. Your arrogance knows no bounds, now that you have broken Shiva's bow. You only regard me as a mantra chanting Brahmin, but I have wrecked havoc on Kings and their families".

Ram then said, "What reason would I have to be proud My Lord? I only touched the bow and it snapped, I did nothing. Regarding offending you, although the descendants of the Raghu Dynasty do not fear even death, the glory of the Brahmins is such that one who bows down to them is freed of all fear. Then how could I offend a Brahmin? Your weapons led us to believe you were a Kshatriya and that's why you were challenged by us".

Hearing this, some change came over the Sage, "String this bow of Vishnu, let me see your prowess", he said as he pulled out another bow and handed it to Ram. To everyone's amazement, the bow seemed to sail into Ram's hands on its own accord. Sage Parshuram recognised the divinity in Ram and declared, "Glory to Sri Ram, the jewel of the Raghu Dynasty, my task on the earth is over. I can leave for Mount Mahendra in peace, while Ram takes on the task of destroying evil on this earth".

At Rishi Parshuram's exit everyone breathed a sigh of relief, the musicians started playing and flowers were showered over Ram. This was the first time I witnessed Ram easing a situation; through the years there would be many situations that Ram would solve through his policy of appeasement, sometimes at great cost to us.

It was late in the afternoon now and we returned to the palace. I was hungry and relieved, too exhausted to be happy. I ate a quick meal and turned into bed only to awake the next day at noon.

Chapter 4
Marriage

Although Ram and I were lawfully man and wife, we had not yet taken the marriage vows and so could not meet each other; this wait seemed endless. According to tradition I was now not to step out of the palace; Uttara as usual would bring me news about what was happening in the city. She reported that there was great excitement in the city, the sweet shops were full of new varieties of sweets, the women went about their work singing songs of blessing for me, people dressed in their best, as if everyday was a festival. In the palace there was frenetic activity in preparation for the actual wedding. I pleaded to have just one look at the merry making in the city and my parents relented. I was allowed a drive through the city in a covered carriage. I couldn't believe what I saw- the entire city was decorated, almost dressed like a bride, the trees were festooned with colourful banners, homes were freshly painted, and the main door of every home was decorated with fresh rangoli[23]

---

23   Patterns on the floor created with flowers, rice powder or chalk.

and strings of mango leaves. Not Janak and Sunaina only, but all of Mithila was celebrating a daughter's wedding, the atmosphere was one of love, yet for me the separation from Ram was unbearable, each day seemed like a year.

After the Swayamwar my father had sent word to King Dashrath to invite him to perform the traditional wedding ceremony and to receive his son's bride. Finally after two weeks, I got news that King Dashrath with his entourage would arrive in Mithila in a couple of hours; senior Ministers had been stationed at the borders of Videha to welcome them into the Kingdom. Ram and Lakshman met up with their father just outside Videha, and re-entered Videha as part of the procession. The procession reached Mithila an hour before sunset; the hour that cows return from their pasture raising great dust in their wake, the hour is thus called 'godhuli'; literally meaning 'cow dust'; this was a good omen since this was regarded as an auspicious hour. They were welcomed with sweets, ornaments, gems and gifts including elephants, horses and cows. My father was at the city gates to welcome King Dashrath and his party to Mithila and escort them to a palace specially built for them.

The procession had to pass the palace to reach its destination; since I was housebound, we girls would have been deprived of the view. Urmila and Uttara pleaded with Rishi Satananda to do something so that we girls too could witness the procession and accordingly my father ordered covered watch towers to be erected along the boundary of the palace garden. Mandavi and Shrutakirti my cousins were with us and so we were about twelve of us; we ran up to the watch towers to watch the procession. I had never seen anything so grand, the people of Mithila had lined the streets, singing and dancing, celebrating the arrival of the wedding procession, the groom of their princess was being formally welcomed. Long before we sighted the procession we heard the kettle drums and the trumpets and then the procession came in view. As the procession passed by, people showered flower petals welcoming the procession. King Dashrath's caparisoned horses led the procession, in a brisk trot, carrying the flag of Ayodhya. Behind them were open chariots laden with gifts from Ayodhya; they were followed by chariots carrying senior ministers and court priests of Ayodhya, and finally came the elephants walking leisurely and swaying to the music. They were caparisoned in red and gold silk, the forehead and upper part of the trunk covered with a golden head gear, encrusted with gems, the end of the tusks had a gold casing; their legs were painted in bright colours, and like the horses, they had bells on their feet. The first elephant, Gajapati, was my father's favourite elephant, seated on him in a golden howdah[24] were King Dashrath and my father. On the howdah fluttered the flags of Ayodhya and Videha. The other three elephants were from Ayodhya, on the second elephant were Ram's two younger brothers, one very much like him; I learnt his name was Bharat and the other one very much like Lakshman, was Shatrughna, the youngest brother. Finally we saw Varalakshmi the cow elephant, the red and gold canopy on her howdah signalled the arrival of the groom. My heart skipped a beat as I saw

---

[24] Seat on an elephant's back which usually has a railing and may have a canopy.

my Ram, dark and handsome waving to the crowds, he was so majestic and there was definitely something divine about him. I hoped he would turn towards the watch tower, but this was not to be. The procession was moving slowly but Varalakshmi seemed to rush past me, alas! Ram was lost from view. From atop the last elephant, ministers from Ayodhya showered coins on the people, reciprocating their welcome. Along the route the elephants were offered bananas which disappeared no sooner than they were offered. The horses were offered jaggery and roasted black chick peas; unlike the elephants, the horses would not eat while 'on duty' and so the riders would accept the offerings. Varalakshmi got a special welcome; since she carried the groom, she was offered turmeric and kumkum, betel leaves, betel nuts and coconuts. She would hold the coconut with her trunk and gently knock it on the ground leaving the broken coconut for the people. I had sent one of the palace boys down with sugar cane pieces for the elephants. I thought I saw Varalakshmi look up at me as she received the sugar cane – imagination can run riot! Once the procession had passed the palace grounds we were summoned back into the palace. The bridegroom had arrived formally so the wedding had now officially begun; the vows would be taken the next morning.

It was the fifth day of the bright fortnight in the month of Margashira[25]; it was my wedding day! Today I would be married to the dark handsome Ram! I was adorned

---

[25] Corresponding to November-December of the Georgian Calendar

with the 'sixteen adornments' or the 'Solah Shringar[26]' of a bride; they cover the bride from head to toe. The 'Solah Shringar' includes decorating the hands and feet with Alta; the wedding dress, flowers in the hair; kohl in the eyes; kumkum and a gold pendant on the forehead. The pendant is secured with a chain that runs along the centre parting of the hair and is secured at the back. All brides have a centre parting which will be later filled with vermillion powder by the groom. Then comes the nose ring; ornaments for the ears; necklaces and chains. Bangles, armbands and rings adorn the hands and a band of gold the waist. The feet are dressed with anklets and finally perfume completes the bride. She receives toe rings and vermillion from her husband. My head was covered with the end of my red and gold saree, and I carried a yellow and gold stole. On the day of the Swayamwar I had butterflies in my stomach as I was dressed; today I was just happy!

Urmila, Mandavi and Shrutakirti wore identical sarees; they were deep pink with intricate gold borders. They had been especially woven by married women for the occasion. When I saw them dressed, I said, "You girls are glowing, you look like brides yourself", promptly one of the ladies took out kohl from her eyes and put a dot behind each one's ear. Sarees had been especially woven for Uttara, Swati and my other friends. Although it was a little cold none of us felt the need to wrap ourselves in warm shawls – "Vanity thy name is Woman!"

---

[26] 'Solah' sixteen and 'Shringar' decoration in Hindi

Uttara was dusky and she looked lovely in an orange saree. I vowed to find her a husband in Ayodhya but that was not to be - she married a soldier in Mithila. Swati was petite and fair and would have looked lovely in any colour but in the light pink saree she reminded me of a rose just bloomed. Unfortunately for us Swati passed away during child birth but her little baby girl survived and she grew up to be as beautiful as her mother.

We got into to the palanquins to go to the wedding pavilion. The strains of the 'Veena[27]' could be heard from our rooms as we waited for King Dashrath and his party to arrive. Five kinds of music would be played for the occasion and soon enough we heard the trumpet which heralded the arrival of the procession, this was followed by the clashing of cymbals, the beating of the kettledrums and the rhythmic clapping of hands. A messenger came to announce the arrival of the procession; my mother and five other married ladies rushed out with lamps to welcome the groom.

I had a few moments to myself and my heart went out to the ladies who could not participate in my wedding celebrations. It was rather unfortunate that women whose husbands had died were not permitted to take part in the ceremonies, they were considered inauspicious. Among those who had been left behind in the palace, was little Saraswati, she was only fifteen; she had lost her husband within a year of her marriage. Saraswati was still a child, had she not been married off she would have been playing

---

[27]   Veena or Vina - a seven stringed musical instrument

with us. She loved wearing long ear danglers and jewellery, but in her husband's passing she would be denied even the small pleasures for the rest of her life; how unfair! What was so inauspicious about this child or in fact any of the ladies whose husbands had died? "Who made these rules and for whom?" I wondered. Men who lost their wives led 'normal' lives and remarried, some even more than once; but for women life was a veritable hell. They could not wear jewellery or bright colours; something we girls had grown up to believe would be part of us always and marriage being the most important event in a girl's life time, loss of a husband was even more traumatic than losing a child. A woman obtained her identity from her father or husband, and when either died, they almost lost their identity; society then looked at them with pity but not always with kindness. I too, was either Janak's daughter or Ram's wife; neither Janaki nor Seeta had an existence without Janak or Ram. There appeared no logic to the many rules and practices imposed by society; and some were plain cruel. Could they not be changed, they were after all man- made rules and my father had once said; "God- made laws, like the rising of the sun in the east and earth's rotation around its axis are not debatable but man- made rules can be changed"; then why wouldn't they, even my father – why wouldn't he do something about this unkindness to women? Maybe as queen I would be able to do something for these women. My reverie was broken with the sound of the conch which meant the welcoming rituals were over and now I would be escorted out. Urmila and the others returned, each one wanting to describe how good Ram looked and how handsome were his brothers, Mandavi especially seemed besotted by Bharat, the brother who looked like Ram, though she played it down quite well. We were now waiting to be called out when we got a message saying my father was calling for my mother and my aunt Ganga, Mandavi and Shrutakirti's mother. "Now what?" was the question in everybody's mind recalling the Sage Parshuram incident at the Swayamwar. Within minutes they were back, all smiles. "What was it?" we all asked in a chorus. My mother sat down and asked for a glass of water; curious and impatient, we urged her to tell. She slowly sipped the water and began after what seemed an eternity. "You see it is like this, after the welcome rituals, the bards began singing the glories of both the dynasties. It was then that King Dashrath learnt of Urmila, Mandavi and Shrutakirti; meanwhile the chief priest of Dashrath, Rishi Vashistha had seen Urmila, Mandavi and Shrutakirti at the welcome rituals and it had crossed his mind that they would make ideal brides for Ram's brothers. After consulting King Dashrath, Rishi Vashistha told our Rishi Satananda that the King of Ayodhya, King Dashrath had asked for the three girls to be married to his other three sons. Your father and uncle thought this was a good idea and wanted to know what both of us thought. Since we too viewed it favourably, looking at Urmila, Mandavi and Shrutakirti, she said, "The three of you are to be married along with Seeta". We were dumbfounded; I, because my words about my three sisters looking like brides had been prophetic; they, because they knew not how to react. "Urmila you are going to be married to Ram's younger brother Lakshman; Mandavi you to Bharat and Shrutakirti your husband will be Shatrughna", announced my mother. Mandavi couldn't stop smiling but the other two were still in a daze. My mother elaborated

"King Dashrath has three wives. Queen Kaushalya, who I believe is a distant cousin of the King, has two children, a daughter Shanta who is married to no other than Rishi Sringi, and a son Ram. Rishi Sringi conducted the yagna for King Dashrath and the King was rewarded with four sons; when the very same Rishi Sringi conducted the yagna for your father; we got two lovely girls. Lakshman and Shatrughna are twins and their mother is Queen Sumitra. Bharat is the son of Queen Kaikeyi who I have been told is the King's favourite Queen".

My mother sent for the bridal jewellery that she had got made along with mine for the other three girls and within the hour there were four brides where there was to have been one! I was left wondering how King Dashrath took a decision to marry off his sons without consulting his wives.

The auspicious time for the wedding vows as determined by the astrologers had arrived and the four of us were led in procession to the wedding pavilion. Later Mandavi told me that Bharat was in a complete state of shock about his wedding since there had never been any talk about his marriage.

The sacred fire was lit and oblations offered to the chanting of Vedic mantras. Then we were offered toe-rings, the most thrilling moment was when Ram removed my head cover to fill my parting with vermilion. Even today when I recall that moment I have goose bumps. The end of my saree was tied to the end of Ram's shawl to signify an indissoluble union. Together we walked around the fire seven times taking the seven wedding vows, now we were man and wife in every sense of the term. There was a grand banquet for everybody after this and fireworks in the evening. Everyday, for as long as we were still in Mithila there were banquets and festivities, to entertain the royal party from Ayodhya. Ever so often King Dashrath would ask to take leave but my father would coax him to stay on for some more time and so we remained in Mithila. Then a message came from Queen Kaikeyi, Bharat's mother asking King Dashrath to return immediately. The earliest date that would be auspicious for us to begin our journey was identified and we began to prepare for Ayodhya.

My father had given us large dowries, elephants, horses, chariots, gold coins, gems, silks and a large retinue of servants. They would all go along with us to Ayodhya. The men would ride horses and we would go in palanquins till the border of Videha after which we would ride in chariots that had arrived from Ayodhya.

The previous afternoon I had taken permission from Ram to visit my parents. When Bharat heard I was going, he asked Mandavi if she would like to go too, in the end all four of us set out. Earlier in the day I had sent a message to my mother saying I might come for lunch and so she should wait for a message from me. She understood well that the message meant, ask father to wait for lunch. I pretended to eat lunch with my husband and father-in-law; my husband ever so perceptive whispered, "You may pretend to the world but not to me; what is it that your mother would have cooked for you?" Finally, the meal was over and we hurried to the palace. This would be the last meal I would have alone with my parents for a long time to come.

My mother took the opportunity of talking to us while waiting for the meal to be served; today we were only the four of us. She asked about our welfare and if we were happy. She told us to remember all that had been ingrained in us during our growing years and reminded us to conduct ourselves in a manner that would bring honour to the house of Janaks. Urmila had suddenly grown up and although she was her usual vivacious self, there was a new maturity about her; today she listened attentively to all that my parents said. Indeed marriage is the beginning of a new chapter in life!

During the meal my father spoke at length on Dharma. "Knowledge of Dharma is not merely the knowledge of values. Dharma is correct application of values. Dharma means the right or righteous thing. It is not in a rigid frame and it changes with the situation. Dharma is appropriateness in thought, action and attitude to a thing or a happening or a desire or an incident in life. Due to its variability it encompasses all situations of all men for all times. Understanding it demands maturity in man, impartiality and honesty, without considerations of convenience. Whether your actions are appropriate or not, is determined by the context of the action - the purpose for which you have uttered the truth or the intention with which you have uttered the untruth. A rigid application of a principle is not Dharma. Dharma is a great flexible principle. An integral part of this Dharma is praying and working for the welfare of the society. Dharma is your accountability to the society's dharma; as queen, people will look up to you as a role model and thus you must think with both head and heart. Always pray to God that he should steer your thoughts correctly and help you keep balance of mind. Do not arrogate to yourself the idea that you with your own judgment can assess the truth. Surrender to the higher power and you won't go wrong".[28]

As I took leave of my parents, my mother hugged me and said, "May compassion, inner strength and forbearance always be your companions in your duty towards your husband, his family and his state"; my father holding me close, his beard tickling my cheek had said, "You will always be my little Janaki even if you become queen of the Universe let alone Ayodhya; you only have to call and your father will respond - remember that always".

---

[28] Unpublished talks of Sadguru K Sivananda Murthy

CHAPTER 5
Life in Ayodhya

I bade farewell to my mother, relatives, friends and maids who had been my constant companions; I didn't know when I would see them again. My father rode along with the procession till the border of Videha where we got into the chariots that had arrived from Ayodhya. The streets were lined with people bidding us farewell as they showered us with flowers and offered us fruit to carry for the journey, my people! There was more than the mere change of mode of transportation, no longer was I Janaki the princess of Videha, I was the future queen of Kosala. Videha would no longer be home, Mithila would no longer beckon me, I would always return as a guest, Ayodhya would be home for ever and ever, but hasn't someone said "don't 'ever' say 'ever'". As I saw my father riding away my eyes welled with tears. I leant over the chariot and watched him ride away. Soon he was a speck and then I could see him no more and I was alone; I cried as I had never cried before and then exhausted, I fell asleep; I awoke when the chariot stopped with a lurch for a night halt; on the fourth day just before sunset we crossed the River Sarayu and entered the Kingdom of Kosala. The Kosala army received us at the border with much fanfare and music. Here I got the first glimpse of how much the soldiers loved my husband; they revered their King Dashrath but loved Ram.

The roads had been sprinkled with water and were decorated with strings of flowers and banners. The fragrance of incense and camphor filled the air. People came out in huge numbers showering us with flowers and vermilion, waving lamps.

I discovered in later years that the Raghu Kings and particularly Ram were much loved and revered all over India. Wherever Ram went, people flocked to pay their respects. In hermitages Rishis welcomed him as their long lost son or disciple, it was as if Ram belonged to everyone.

We left the night camp early the next morning; we had to deck ourselves again as brides in readiness for the palace welcome. It had been warming up from the time we left Mithila and today was a particularly warm day, but as we neared Ayodhya almost everybody had left their homes, braving the heat to welcome us. I was nervous yet excited. There were welcome arches at the entrance of Ayodhya festooned with banners and flowers. I had finally entered Ayodhya welcomed by throngs of people. When we left that morning my husband came specially to tell me that no sooner we entered Ayodhya I was to begin looking to my right and I would see the top of the palace. When we entered Ayodhya I was amazed at the sheer size of the city. They were wide stone flagged roads, the roads were lined with flowering trees and along the roads there were benches for people to sit. I passed many gardens full of flowers.

I saw huge buildings nothing like I had seen in Videha, actually even the women and children in Ayodhya seemed bigger than those in Videha. As I was taking in all that, I saw something to the right that looked liked a snow clad mountain glistening in the sun. The sun was high and I had to squint to see what it was; I gasped! This was no mountain, it was the palace of King Dashrath, as we neared it, the palace disappeared behind the trees. We entered the palace gates, arches of banana leaves had been erected at regular intervals and the entire driveway was festooned with strings of flowers and banners. The driveway was so long that it took us quite a while to get to the palace. I was tired after the long journey and now nervous at meeting my mothers-in-law. Although Ram was the son of the eldest queen, Queen Kaushalya, he had told me he regarded the others as his mothers and I too should regard them with the same love I would regard his mother.

We passed under a huge arch and in front of me was the palace; a huge four-storeyed structure, plastered in white and glistening in the sun, I was awestruck at the sheer size; I am sure all of Mithila could have been accommodated here. The chariot rumbled into a cobbled courtyard and halted at the main door. Ram, Lakshman, Bharat and Shatrughna were already there waiting for us. We walked in a slow procession over a carpet of flowers - at the threshold were four traditional pots filled with rice, one for each of us, we had to tip this over the threshold into the house with our right foot. This ritual was symbolic of a bride bringing with her prosperity into her new home.

The veil covering my face was lifted and I was greeted by a regal lady in a sea green brocade saree, she was Queen Kaushalya. She had well defined features, was fairer than her son and had a lovely smile. She waved a tray with a lamp and camphor around Ram and me, as we prostrated at her feet to receive her blessings she said, "Seeta this is your home and I will be your mother now; I wish all happiness for you and my son". Behind her was Queen Sumitra in a sky blue brocade saree, she was shorter than Mother Kaushalya and plump but a more gentle face I had never seen. I could see her love for Ram as she performed the welcome rituals and then we had to wait for Bharat's mother Queen Kaikeyi who was still getting dressed to receive us. She arrived wearing an orange and gold saree. I was rather amused that she was preoccupied adjusting the danglers in her ears with one hand while waving the lamp around us with the other.

Over the next couple of weeks we settled into the palace routine. Everything here was much grander both in scale and by way of protocol, it would take a little time getting used to this style. Ram was a wonderful husband; he would explain to me the ways of the palace. My husband spent his entire day at the court, as the eldest son he would be King after his father, and was being groomed for that role. Ram was also King Dashrath's favourite child, and the King could never begin his day without greeting Ram. Should Ram have been even a minute later than expected, King Dashrath would send someone looking for him. Invariably Ram would be helping someone out of a situation, it could be an unpaid debt, or a quarrel over land rights; people believed Ram could help them out and he did. He said

"With them I use my head and heart; for myself only my head".

My husband and I grew closer to each other with each passing day, the love at first sight seemed to grow deep roots and new shoots, there was always something new to discover about each other. In the evenings my husband and I would take a walk into the city, we mingled with the people and they would talk to us freely. Each day we walked a different route covering every quarter in the city. Ram and I toured the entire kingdom of Kosala, where ever we went my husband made it a point to interact with the common man and expected me to interact with the women and together we understood their lives, their hopes and aspirations and their challenges. Ram thus knew the ground realities and could address their problems appropriately. That he would be King was taken for granted and he was given due respect; Lakshman, Bharat and Shatrughna were regarded as elder brothers. Over time I too developed a bond with the people, the love and respect was mutual. To some I was a daughter, to some a mother and to others a sister.

Ram and I could spend hours together on our own. I never tired of listening to him describing his adventures in the forest with Rishi Vishwamitra. He told me how he and Lakshman had killed the demoness Tadaka. I knew it was Ram who had killed her but he was so magnanimous, since Lakshman was with him and an excellent marksman, he gave Lakshman equal credit. Ram was at first hesitant to use force against Tadaka because she was a lady; Rishi Vishwamitra then told him that as a Kshatriya it was his duty to protect 'Dharma' and by punishing the person in 'adharma' he saved that person from unrighteousness."

Ram also told me how, as they walked past Rishi Gautam's Ashram, Ahalya sprang to life. My sweet husband omitted the fact that Ahalya was freed of a curse when the dust from his feet touched the stone in which Ahalya was trapped.

Another common interest was playing chess - in Mithila I would often play with my father and that had helped to hone my skills. I could often checkmate Ram and would feel terrible about it. Why? Because I was brought up within the framework that men – father, brother, husband or son are always stronger, more intelligent and more capable than mother, sister, wife or daughter! And my being able to checkmate my husband was against unwritten rules. My husband wasn't unduly concerned about being checkmated and could not understand my distress, "Seeta", he would implore, 'this is a game, just like the game of life; play the game and play it well – that's all about it. Now get me something to eat".

I had discovered a Shiva temple not far from the palace and the two of us would visit the temple early in the morning. We offered water to our dear Shiva. On the thirteen night and fourteenth day of the month of Phalgun[29] we celebrated Mahashivratri; this is the great night of the Lord Shiva, and my husband who loved Lord Shiva and took part in all the festivities.

---

[29] Last month of the Hindu calendar corresponding to February-March of the Georgian Calendar.

Soon the mango trees flowered, the fragrance wafted into my room at the break of dawn and those were the times that I longed to be back in Mithila, but the feeling would pass. The mango flowers gave way to the fruit; I loved the sharp taste of the raw mango. Ram loved it too; he would pluck a mango, break off the stem and rub the mango against the bark of the tree to remove the bitter sap. He then broke the tender mango with the side of his palm and we would sprinkle salt and red chilly powder and smack our lips relishing the mango.

Phalgun was followed by Chaitra[30], on the ninth day of the bright fortnight of the month of Chaitra was Ram's birthday - he would be eighteen this year. His birthday was celebrated with the palace being lit up in the evening and a grand banquet for over a thousand guests. Mother Kaushalya gave away clothes and food to the poor, although the Kingdom of Kosala in general and Ayodhya in particular were prosperous, there were always needy people. That morning when Ram and I went to the temple I carried a saree, green bangles and vermilion for Mother Parvati, it was difficult to think of what to take for the Lord since he is always in meditation and is satisfied with cold water and so I took with me his favourite fruit – the humble Ber.[31] The Ber tree grows wild and is found all over North India, without any special human care it produces abundant fruit which apart from tasting good is packed with nutrients.

---

[30] First Month of the Hindu Calendar, corresponding to March-April of the Georgian Calendar

[31] *Zizyphus vulgaris:* It is also known as the Indian jujube and has an astringent taste.

Just before we retired that night, my husband gave me a ruby studded peacock pendant which hung on a thick gold chain; as he put it round my neck he said for the first time "I love you Seeta, you are very precious to me, and I will not be able to spend a day without you". I hugged him and said, "I promise you, you will never have to spend a day without me, I will not even go to Mithila without you, and I will never take this off". I had to know how he got the necklace, he would have been too embarrassed to ask Mother Kaushalya to order it much less order it himself. Sheepishly he said, "I told Mother Sumitra that I wanted to give you something, an unusual piece of jewellery and she did the rest for me".

We sisters would spend the mornings with our mothers-in-law; we learnt from them the traditions of the family and decorum of the inner palace. Each of them told us their sons' likes and dislikes with regard to food. Mother Kaushalya told me that while Ram would never make a demand he wanted his food hot – just off the pan. Mother Sumitra told me that he loved white butter and sugar and so I made sure that it was there for every meal till he gently told me that butter and sugar at the evening meal is enough. Queen Kaikeyi told me that Ram loved mango pickle. I wondered who would tell our husbands what we girls liked, - or was that not important?

The one thing that delighted the mothers was to tell us stories about their sons' childhood. Stories about their own families were very sketchy. Once when I asked Mother Sumitra, who was the princess of Magadh, about her childhood, she didn't have anything to say except that she had very kind parents and that she led a happy life. Had I been asked that question I could have talked for hours about my growing years and my wonderful parents, but nobody asked!

I asked Mother Kaushalya about my husband's sister Shanta, she had not been able to attend my wedding and so we had not yet met. She told me in a no-nonsense way how it was necessary to give up Shanta in adoption. Shanta was born with a disability in her leg, a cause attributed to the fact that Dashrath and Kaushalya's was a consanguineous marriage as they were cousins. On the advice of the Chief Priest of Kosala, Rishi Vashistha, the child was given in adoption to the King of Angadesha, Romapada and in due course Shanta was healed of the disability. Her adoptive father then married her to Rishi Sringi, who later conducted a yagna for Dashrath to beget sons.

Shanta was close to both sets of parents and when she was wedded to Rishi Sringi a large part of her dowry was provided by King Dashrath. Shanta now lived with her husband in Sringverpur on the banks of the River Ganga. Mother Sumitra added that Shanta resembled Mother Kaushalya and was as gentle.

Mother Kaushalya and Mother Sumitra were always together, Mother Sumitra loved Mother Kaushalya as one would love a mother. She would do nothing without consulting Mother Kaushalya. I loved them dearly, of Mother Kaikeyi I was in awe, although she showered the four of us with affection.

My father-in-law too was concerned about us and would always ask Ram if I was happy and tell him to make sure that all my needs were met. Nevertheless, I was rather confused with the many sides of the King's personality. One personality I saw was King Dashrath in court, this was a towering personality both revered and respected; the other was father Dashrath – concerned, compassionate and always available for his children; in another aspect, as the besotted lover, Dashrath completely threw me off balance. Queen Kaikeyi and the King even in company conducted themselves as if there was nobody around; given that my own parents' conduct was sober and restrained I was rather bewildered at her coquetry and his response! Much later I realised that I was uncomfortable with this behaviour because I had grown to love King Dashrath as my own father, and for me 'fathers could not be lovers'. I looked back at myself over the years rather amused at my innocence. At that point in time there was of course no question of discussing it with anybody; not even Urmila. Was it this or was it something else that disturbed me? I could never put my finger on the nagging disturbance till much later.

Ram had been very keen to spend time with the Rishi Vashistha and no sooner had the Sage returned from his meditation in the Himalayas, both of us paid a visit to the hermitage.

The Rishi lived with his wife Arundhati on the outskirts of Ayodhya. Arundhati was known for her piety and single minded devotion to her husband. Once there was a great drought on the earth for twelve years. The Rishis living in the Himalayas were also affected by the famine created by this drought. Arundhati then sat down in intense meditation;

Shiva pleased with her devotion and determination brought down rain on the earth.

It was here that my husband and his brothers had spent their formative years. Arundhati was a mother to them during this time and loved them like her own. Lakshman and Bharat had often said that Ram and Shatrughna were her favourites and she would serve them food before anyone else.

Arundhati served us a simple lunch of rice and vegetables; I had never before tasted any food with such subtle and delicate flavours. Ram said that the vegetables and rice grown in the hermitage imbibed the spiritual vibrations of the Rishi and his wife and so tasted 'divine'. The Sage and Ram got talking and Arundhati took me around the hermitage. She seemed to read my confused mind and gently said, "In this world of duality we will be continually called upon to face situations and challenges that we could not even dream of. Remember then that nothing happens without the will of God; which means this is part of his plan and nothing happens without a greater reason. Without the experience, you wouldn't grow into who you are meant to be. The past has gone, the future is wrapped in mystery, what we have in the present is this instant. I bless you my child that you may live up to the challenges that life throws up for you, but this instant the sun is shining and there is happiness". I felt much better, just then the Rishi and Ram walked up to us in the garden. We took our leave promising to return soon.

Some months later Mother Kaikeyi's brother Prince Yudhajit had come on a visit to Ayodhya and wanted take Bharat and Mandavi back with him. Bharat and Shatrughna were inseparable and so it was agreed that Bharat, Mandavi, Shatrughna and Shrutakirti would leave with Bharat's uncle the next morning. Something was gnawing at me as I wished them a safe journey the next day.

One afternoon when Ram returned for lunch he told me my parents would be arriving later in the evening. I looked at him unbelieving, he then told me how King Dashrath had heard that King Janak and Queen Sunaina would pass close to the border of Kosala and had sent his trusted minister Sumantra with a carriage to escort them to Ayodhya. My eyes filled with tears at the kindness of my father-in-law. As I grew older I realised that unlike the classical languages that have a set number of words and a formal grammar to ensure uniformity in comprehension; the language of love is unique to each individual; only the speaker and the spoken understand the language.

According to custom, girls' parents would seldom visit their daughter's matrimonial home and then too only if invited by their son-in-law. My parents were on their way back to Mithila after a pilgrimage, but would not come to Ayodhya since they had not been invited. They had not informed King Dashrath of their passing by, lest it appear that they were seeking an invitation. Sensitive to their hesitation and the longing of parents to meet their daughters, the King had taken it upon himself to bring my parents to Ayodhya with due protocol – how sweet was that!

My mother met my mothers-in-law for the first time and they seemed to meet like old friends. My mother was so happy to see her daughters living in a grand palace surrounded by people who loved them. When she left, she said, "I am grateful to God for all that he has given my daughters; my duty towards my children is over. Seeta and Urmila, it is now in your hands to make a success of your lives".

CHAPTER 6

The Coronation that Wasn't

Ram and Lakshman had gone to settle a dispute in a nearby town; they returned late in the morning and my husband was getting ready to attend court which was in progress. He had some moments before he left; as we sat chatting he told me about an old man whom he had met in the morning. The man had lost his leg when he fell off a tree; he had no one to care for him yet was happy and cheerful. "How would you define happiness?" I asked. Ram said, "Happiness is a state of mind, it is subjective, and differs from person to person and is relative to a context. Most of us believe that the satisfaction of material needs and desires will lead to happiness. Happiness does not lie in the objects of the outside world; it is an experience of a state of contentment. However, happiness is mental and refers to the mind and so is temporary. 'Bliss' is the highest form of happiness. Bliss is that of the soul, the consciousness. If the bliss of the consciousness is achieved the causeless happiness of the mind is experienced"[32]. Just then a messenger came

---

[32] Unpublished talks of Sadguru K Sivananda Murthy

in to say Rishi Vashistha was there to see him. Ram sprang up and rushed out to receive him, I was rather surprised at the visit, I was sure that the cause of the visit was significant else the Sage would have sent for Ram.

They talked for about an hour, and when the Sage left, Ram returned with a perplexed expression. "My father with the consent of the court has decided to declare to the people that I will be the heir apparent and tomorrow will be the coronation", he said in a flat emotionless tone. Although this was to be, yet I was quite pleased to hear of it, but couldn't understand my husband's lack of enthusiasm; after all he had been groomed for this position, it was a logical step, although I wondered why it couldn't wait for when Bharat and Shatrughna returned.

Almost to himself he said, "It's not fair! The four of us – Lakshman, Bharat, Shatrughna and I have always done things together, we were born almost together, we studied together, fate had us even marry together, and now I have been singled out for this honour. It isn't their fault that they were born after me. Not just they but even their progeny will not beget this honour of becoming King of Kosala; I cannot reconcile myself to this injustice. What is more, the entire court has agreed to this. I thought father's ministers were wise and just. The Kingdom should have been divided equally amongst the four of us".

Turning to me he said, "Now that the decision has been taken, there is nothing more to be said. Rishi Vashistha has asked me to follow a regimen till the coronation is over; this includes observing celibacy, sleeping on a mat on the ground and being on a diet of fruit and milk and that too only for bare sustenance. Through this period we are to have minimum conversation and spend our time in meditation. You get things organised and I will go and inform mother. You might wonder at the suddenness of things, but apparently the planets will be in favourable positions tomorrow and after that this configuration will not occur for some months, so the ceremony will have to go on without Bharat and Shatrughna, I am going to miss them". Ram was so self effacing that he was almost embarrassed at being officially declared the heir apparent.

As the news spread I heard the drums and the trumpets as the people celebrated, the shouts of "Victory to Ram" rent the air. My husband was being crowned as the next King of Kosala, it was official! I was happy for both of us. While my husband was away, I quickly ran through my wardrobe and identified the saree and jewellery I would wear; had my husband known he would not have approved my being preoccupied with dressing when I should have been in contemplation.

Ram returned with Mother Kaushalya and Mother Sumitra, they blessed us both and initiated our fast by feeding us with their hands; the two decided they would fast as well for our well being. Once we were alone Ram was silent and in meditation, I too sat down to meditate but was often distracted by the sounds of the merrymaking that wafted in from the city. I thanked the Lord Shiva and Mother Parvati for giving us this opportunity to serve our people. I assured them that neither of us would waver from the path of dharma and surrendered to them to keep us on the path.

The next morning we awoke at the crack of dawn and were bathed and dressed for the morning rituals of the coronation. At about eight o'clock a messenger came with a message from Sumantra summoning Ram to Mother Kaikeyi's palace. I was rather surprised since it was nearing the time that Ram should have been leaving for the temple before proceeding to the court for the coronation.

I dressed and waited to be called but there was no word from anybody, there was something different in the air. There was no sound of revelry unlike the previous day; in fact there was dead silence. I was at a loss as to what to do. So I just sat and waited, I was getting restless but couldn't show it to the retainers, later I realised this was just an introduction to my period of 'waiting'. At about noon Ram returned in the same state as he had left, quite clearly he had not participated in any of the rituals. He told me in the same expressionless voice of the day before, "My father wants me to spend fourteen years in the forest and I must leave immediately". "What!" I exclaimed, my husband gave me an exasperated look and repeated what he had said earlier.

I burst into tears, because something must have gone horribly wrong; Ram said 'he' must leave immediately not 'we' and for fourteen years! What had happened to the coronation? My husband wiped my tears and although he seemed to be in a hurry, sat me down and told me what had happened.

"When I reached the palace this morning I saw Rishi Vashistha and Sumantra speaking to each other in hushed tones; when I asked them what had happened they merely pointed to the inner chamber. I walked in and was horrified to see father lying on the floor bathed in perspiration and writhing in pain. Mother Kaikeyi was in the room and when she tried to help him, he pushed her away. I knelt down to help him up but he held me in his arms and clinging to me wept like a child, saying "I'm sorry my son, please forgive me". I couldn't fathom what was going on. I looked towards Mother Kaikeyi for an explanation, she said, "He wants to tell you something but he is unable to do so".

I said, "Mother if you know what he wants to convey to me, why don't you tell me". Mother then said to me, "Long years ago I accompanied your father on the battlefield when he was fighting a demon by the name Shambhasura. Shambhasura's arrow struck your father in the chest, it was a deep wound and your father was bleeding profusely. At the same instant a rain of arrows broke the chariot wheel. I managed to repair the wheel and drove your father off the battle field. The army was able to carry on the fight and killed the demon. Meanwhile with God's grace your father recovered. As a token of gratitude for saving the Kingdom of Kosala and his own life, your father gave me two boons of my choice. Since at that point in time I could have asked for nothing more than your father's life I said I would ask for them later at an appropriate time; today I am asking for them that's all".

"And what were those boons?" I asked.

She said candidly, "I would like the throne of Kosala for Bharat and you to go into the forest for fourteen years".

When I heard this I said, "If that is what you want I am prepared to do it, where is the issue? Father is devastated, not so much because Mother Kaikeyi has demanded the throne for her son Bharat, but because he and I will be separated; and for him this is unbearable. Unfortunately for him he is left with no choice. He told Mother Kaikeyi that he would readily agree to the first demand, that of Bharat being coronated; with regard to the second demand, my poor father with folded hands pleaded with Mother Kaikeyi not to insist he be separated from me. However, Mother was in no mood to relent and we of the Raghu dynasty keep our word even if it means death. It killed me to see the great Dashrath groveling at his wife's feet; it was such a painful scene I pray no son ever has to go through this experience of seeing his father in such grief."

Ram continued "To go back further so that you fully appreciate the situation, since Mother Kaushalya and Mother Sumitra had not borne an heir to the throne my father was advised to take yet another wife. This was Mother Kaikeyi the daughter of the King Ashwapati of Kaikeya. When my father married Mother Kaikeyi he promised her father that Mother Kaikeyi's son would inherit the throne; he could make this promise since both the senior queens had been unable to fulfil this duty of theirs towards the Kingdom of Kosala. However with my birth as the eldest son, it was assumed that this chapter was closed. Clearly it wasn't so, when Mother Kaikeyi heard about the coronation she asked father for the two boons and father readily agreed, I am sure he could never have imagined that she would ask for the throne for Bharat, much less have me banished from the kingdom".

"I am neither sorry for not being coronated nor for having to go into the forest. What is fourteen years in the life time of a man? But I am rather hurt about Mother Kaikeyi's treatment of the man she claims to love."

I couldn't help saying, "The boons were her right and she must have them, but with every right isn't there a corresponding duty?"

Ram replied tersely, "It is not for us to define somebody else's dharma, we must follow our own dharma and now I must depart to the forest, the sooner the better".

"What do you mean 'I'? What about me?" I cried, to which my husband said," You stay here in the palace and look after my parents. The forest is not a place for a princess. There will be wild animals, the climate will be harsh either very cold or very hot, if you get by the cold and heat you will not be able to deal with the rains, during the rains there are scorpions and leeches on the ground, life will not be comfortable for you. There will be no chariots, you will have to walk through rough terrain, and you will have to cook, fetch water and sleep on the cold hard floor. You cannot come with me, moreover I am going as a hermit, and you will be a distraction, stay here comfortably and wait for my return".

I could not bear the thought of my husband wandering alone in the forest, how could I live comfortably in a palace when my husband was wandering all alone in unknown forests? That Ram who was waited upon hand and foot by his wife and a battalion of retainers; how could I let him go all alone, he would not be able to take care of himself. I said, "It is not only my duty but my right to be with my husband. I will walk behind you, Lord Shiva and Mother Parvati will protect me, I know how to cook, I can sleep on the floor. If you leave me behind I will die, I cannot live without you. Please, I beseech you take me along. I'm telling you, I'll die without you". My husband looked into my eyes, he had tears in his eyes when he said, "Come along my Seeta, I too can't live without you. But get out of this finery. We have to go as hermits and take the vow of celibacy".

Get out of the finery! I would have been happy to wear rags, as long as I was with Ram! Mother Kaikeyi and her boons meant nothing any more; anybody could have been King as long as we were not separated. I asked him if he had told Mother Kaushalya; he nodded, he had given her this news in the gentlest possible way, my sweet husband! He told her that instead of becoming King of Kosala, he was now King of the Forests! At first Mother Kaushalya was shocked and said she couldn't bear to live without Ram; but she quickly recovered and said that time would pass quickly and she would wait for his return. I marvelled at my husband's attitude, although he had the divine spark in him, he was after all human and must have been or rather should have been disappointed; but for my husband - his duty was above everything else and he was being a dutiful son; as he had earlier said, I think with head and heart for others and for myself only with my head.

We now had to go to Mother Kaushalya's palace and take her leave; she was aghast that I had decided to accompany my husband and that he had agreed. She tried to dissuade me using all her persuasive skills. She said that it was not a good omen if the 'Lakshmi' of the house left, how could she manage the palace without me; I had to think of my sisters. It would not have been proper for either Ram or me to engage with her so I stared at my toes and my husband stood by me in silence. Mother ultimately realised that I was not going to change my mind and I had my husband's support.

As we were leaving for Mother Sumitra's palace, Lakshman arrived on the scene, his face white as a sheet. "What is this that I hear?" My husband briefly told him what had happened. Lakshman turned red with anger, "This is the work of Manthara. Mother Kaikeyi is not capable of this intrigue- she is too full of herself. Anyway now that it has happened there is precious little we can do about it. I am accompanying you into the forest".

Manthara was a wizened old hunchback who had been Mother Kaikeyi's wet nurse and had accompanied her to Ayodhya. She had a sharp tongue and was cunning and scheming, she was the one person in the palace who was universally disliked; but the code of conduct of the Raghu Dynasty would not permit this feeling to be expressed, much less discussed.

Ram knew that if he had refused his brother permission, Lakshman would have been devastated. However, Ram did not want Lakshman to leave Urmila and accompany us to the forest. He asked Lakshman to take Mother Sumitra's permission in the hope that she would refuse. Mother Sumitra was wise; she knew if she had refused Lakshman permission he would have remained in a sullen mood which was not a happy thought and at the end of the day everybody and particularly Urmila would have been miserable. I think she also felt that both Mother Kaushalya and she would be at peace now that Lakshman was there to take care of Ram and me. She gave him her blessings asking him to serve Ram and me as his parents. How wise that was, in one sentence she gave Lakshman a status in the group that was departing for the forest, otherwise he would have seen himself as an appendage to us. Urmila expected that she too would be accompanying us, but when Urmila was told she was to stay back she was stunned, my little vivacious sister just stared at us with vacant eyes.

Ram, Lakshman and I went to Queen Kaikeyi's palace to take leave of the King. Waiting there were Bhagirathi Sumantra's wife and Arundhati the wife of Sage Vashistha. Arundhati's words at the hermitage – "In this world of duality we will be continually called upon to face situations and challenges that we could not even dream of"; came rushing back to me. Both of them tried to convince me to change my mind, but I stared at my toes and Ram stood beside me in silence, they too realised my resolve and finally accepted my going.

As we stepped into the inner chamber, the King, my father-in-law continued to lie stretched on the floor. His clothes were dishevelled, his hair uncombed, he was unshaven and weeping copiously. I couldn't believe my eyes. I had never seen my father-in-law other than formally dressed, and now this! There could be no better example to illustrate what attachment can do to a person. My father-in-law's attachment to Kaikeyi and to Ram had brought him down to his knees. I felt so sorry for him, yet wondered, how did King Dashrath of Ayodhya allow himself to come to this? I was not convinced that "keeping his word to his wife" was the issue. I believed then and always that the King was so enraptured by Queen Kaikeyi that he could not have borne the torture of her emotional and physical withdrawal had he put his foot down. My indignation had nothing to do with our sent being away for fourteen years; I couldn't have cared less about the coronation. But I was aghast at how the passion and attachment of one man could affect the destiny of so many people!

Queen Kaikeyi and Manthara had the robes of renunciation made of the bark of trees and deer skin ready for us. When Rishi Vashistha saw them, he was furious. I heard him raise his voice for the first time; "Maithili is not a renunciate and will not wear robes of a renunciate", he boomed. Everybody was stunned; nobody had heard Rishi Vashistha ever raise his voice. Sumantra stood by the Sage and said, "No civilised society strips their women of their ornaments; how do you expect us to face the King of Videha who has given us his daughter in the firm belief that we will protect her. Vaidehi will wear her ornaments, don't stretch yourself that far Mother Kaikeyi". This seemed to have some effect on my father-in-law, he sat up and in his old familiar voice commanded Ram to ensure that I carried with me all my ornaments. He then went into a swoon, as we prostrated at his feet, and fell on the floor. There was pin drop silence and then Sumantra led the way out to the carriage that awaited us. Rishi Vashistha accompanied us out where we were joined by Arundhati, Bhagirathi and the wives of other Ministers; as Ram and I prostrated at their feet, Rishi Vashistha looked at me with such tenderness that I almost burst into tears.

As I was stepping out over the threshold, the very same threshold over which a few years back I had tipped a measure of rice symbolising the prosperity I would bring into my matrimonial home, Urmila clung to my feet and wept, "Don't leave me, please take me with you", she cried. Lakshman told her that she would be a distraction since he was going to serve his brother. I could neither say anything nor do anything for her; I just looked down and walked on. Mother Sumitra then gathered Urmila in her arms and led her away. Urmila's stricken face haunted me for a long time and for many years after that I would wake up in the middle of the night, Urmila's cries ringing in my ears; I wondered if she would ever forgive me for leaving her behind.

Mother Kaushalya and Mother Sumitra came to see us off; composed and dignified; they showered rice grains on our head and blessed us. Mother Kaushalya handed to Ram and Lakshman their signet rings, saying "It is extremely inauspicious to remove them, this is not an ornament, this is the protection that the Raghu Dynasty offers you." I was numb and cannot recall any emotion; my husband was quiet and Lakshman grim. As the carriage rolled out, Sage Vashistha and the entire court walked with us, there was not a dry eye. Just then we heard my father-in-law call to Sumantra who was in the driver's seat. Lakshman and I turned to look and sure enough he had got up and was now urging us to return. Ram sat as if he were a statue and asked Sumantra to move faster. Sumantra was hesitant saying that it would amount to disobedience and he would have to answer the King later. Ram told him to say that he, Sumantra, didn't hear the King's voice in the din, so Sumantra cracked the whip and we moved quickly.

As we left the palace gates we saw all of Ayodhya on the streets, weeping and wailing- they couldn't believe Ram was leaving them. Through the sound of wails I heard men and women curse both Queen Kaikeyi and Manthara; I covered my ears, I did not want to hear any of it.

The city followed us, people begging their Ram to return. Ram sat composed urging Sumantra to drive faster, yet the crowd did not give up, they ran behind the chariot and followed us till sunset when we had reached the banks of the River Tamsa, south of Ayodhya. We settled here for the night; when everybody was asleep, we got into the chariot and drove into the night. Ram told Sumantra to drive in such a way that people would not be able to follow our tracks. So Sumantra went zigzagging through the forest till we reached the banks of the River Gomti. After crossing the Vedashruti and Syandika rivers we reached Sringverpur on the banks of the River Ganga. On the way Sumantra narrated to Ram the instructions he had received from King Dashrath. The King had told Sumantra to drive with us in the forests for a few days after which he was to take us back to Ayodhya. His sons, the King said, were strong headed like himself, and may not choose to return; in that case Sumantra should return to Ayodhya with me. What the King did not know was that I was as strong willed as his sons!

CHAPTER 7
Chitrakoot

At the sight of the mighty Ganga my heart leapt with joy, how peacefully yet powerfully she flowed towards the sea, where she would become one with the infinite ocean - the ultimate goal of our lives to merge with the infinite. I felt so calm and peaceful in her presence, I felt as though she had absorbed all our trials and tribulations and left behind peace.

The entire region was known as Sringverpur, my husband's sister Shanta and her husband, Rishi Sringi lived here, but this was not the time to meet them. The Nishads lived nearby and hearing that Ram had come, their chieftain, Guha came with his people to pay his respects, he invited us to his village; we could not accept his hospitality since Ram and along with him Lakshman had taken the vows of renunciation; so Guha asked his people to come and receive Ram's blessing, they came laden with fruit, they spent some time with us and then returned to their village. Guha stayed back to serve us. We met Guha for the first time when we arrived at Sringverpur, but within hours we discovered a devoted friend. That night was spent under a tree on the outskirts of Guha's habitation; next morning we would cross the Ganga, and truly begin our Vanvas – or life in the forest.

Ram now asked Sumantra to return to Ayodhya; Sumantra repeated the King's message but Ram gently but firmly told him that he, Ram, would not be following his dharma if he returned. He told Sumantra to tell his father not to be too distressed, fourteen years would pass swiftly and Bharat was capable of ruling Kosala. He gave Sumantra the responsibility of taking care of not only his father, but also of Ayodhya. At this point Lakshman joined in and said to Sumantra, "What a paradox this is, normally it is the practice for a king to go to the forest for meditation after handing over the kingdom to his son, here it is just the other way round." My husband silenced Lakshman and told Sumantra that Lakshman's remark should be expunged from his memory. Sumantra then turned to me entreating me to return with him, again I stared at my toes but Ram asked me to give Sumantra an appropriate response. I said, "Please ask my in-laws to forgive my disobedience, but I want to follow the dharma of a wife and serve my husband," I thought that was short and sweet!

Sumantra bowed to Ram and with tears in his eyes turned the carriage around and sped to Ayodhya. I wondered what was going on in his mind, as he drove back to Ayodhya with an empty carriage.

We now needed a boat to cross the Ganga; there was only one boat in sight, Ram called out to Kevat the lone boatman to ferry us across the river. He sauntered up to

us, and said that he could not take us across since he had
heard that there was some magic about the dust on Ram's
feet, that transformed whatever it came into contact with,
into a woman. "Get us another boatman who does not
believe in magic", Lakshman snapped. Kevat shrugged and
pointed out that there were no boats in sight. Lakshman was
exasperated but had no option but to ask Kevat, "So what
is the solution?" Kevat then said, "If you allow me to wash
Ram's feet, I'll wash off the dust and then you may step into
the boat and I'll ferry you across the river". Ram smiled,
washing another's feet was a way of according great respect,
under normal circumstances Ram would not have allowed
Kevat to touch his feet, but now Ram had no choice. Kevat
lovingly washed Ram's feet and the three of us got into the
boat. Guha insisted on accompanying us; he said he would
build us our hut in the forest and once he saw us settled
he would return. No sooner had we left the banks, than
numerous boats appeared from nowhere. Lakshman looked
at Kevat questioningly; sheepishly Kevat said, "My Lord if
I had allowed the other boats into the river I would never
have got the opportunity of washing your brother's feet."
My husband laughed and Lakshman grit his teeth. Kevat
deposited us on the other side, but we had no money to pay
him. I offered one of my rings in lieu of money, but Kevat
refused; he said he'd wait for us and take the payment on our
return; our indebtedness to him was the best way to ensure
our return, he must have thought!

As we walked through the forest I got my first taste of
'forest life'; we walked in file along a well beaten mud path,
Ram in front, Lakshman at the back along with Guha,

and I remained in the centre. This was how we walked, thereafter as well. Thorns scratched my arms and my saree got entangled in the nettles so I covered my arms with the loose end of my saree and held my saree close to my body, and I was just fine. We spent another night under a tree, I was amazed at myself, I was coping brilliantly, earlier I had managed to escape the nettles and now had slept fast and woken up fresh, never before had I slept so well! We set out before the sun rose and reached the confluence of the Rivers Ganga, Yamuna and Saraswati at Prayag at sunrise; we took a dip in the waters and set off again.

After a couple of hours of walking, in the distance, we saw a spire of smoke, Ram said it was Rishi Bhardwaj's hermitage. We halted outside the gate and Ram called out to one of the disciples working in the garden and said, "Son please tell the Rishi that Ram, Lakshman and Seeta are here". This was the protocol; one did not enter a hermitage without being invited. Minutes later the Rishi came rushing out, he knew how and why we were there. Sages have divine sight and know what is going on anywhere and at anytime. He welcomed us in and his disciples offered us water, fruits and milk. Rishi Bhardwaj insisted that we spend the night at the hermitage and the next morning he would send a guide to lead us further ahead. I was relieved at the invitation; I was tired and the soles of my feet were sore and covered with blisters. I had never walked so much and certainly never barefoot. The Rishi gave me some oil for my feet and almost like magic the blisters disappeared and after a night's rest I was refreshed and ready to go.

Next morning we set out, southwards again, with four disciples accompanying us. Two led the party and the other two along with devoted Guha, made up the rear of this small procession. Ram was talking to the two in front and Lakshman to the boys at the back; ever so often they would switch places so that they had the opportunity to hear both the brothers. I overheard Ram talking to them about 'surrender to God'.

He said, "Surrender is understanding and believing that the success of the result, the result of the action and the intention of the action are all 'His'. If you have surrendered, asking stops. Complaints cease. Every thing is accepted as His 'Grace'". "Surrender is the unshakable belief that you belong to Him and He to you. It is the height of unperturbability. It is a readiness to be destroyed. It is maturity without expectations. It is a courage, which does not depend on hope. It is the destination. It is the farthest that man can go". "Know and accept that whatever happens is according to the will of God and with the permission of your Guru. This is surrender; this is the passport to Jnana or true knowledge".[33]

I recalled Arundhati saying the same thing – 'Nothing happens without the will of God'. I now realised that Ram was always so composed and relaxed because he had surrendered.

When we reached the banks of the River Yamuna, Ram asked the boys to return to the hermitage; they agreed only

---

[33] Unpublished talks of Sadguru K Sivananda Murthy

when Ram promised them that he would meet them in Ayodhya, fourteen years from the day. Ram and Lakshman took a dip in the river and we crossed the river on a raft crafted by Lakshman. The people living on the other bank looked on us curiously, wondering who we were and where we were headed; I must have looked strange, decked in jewellery but barefoot. They were members of the forest tribes the Bhils and the Gonds who do not look upon city dwellers entering the forest, kindly; so although we would have rather not told people our story, Lakshman explained to them who we were and what brought us to their land. On hearing our story, their curiosity turned to sympathy, their leader, said it was not safe to travel through the forest particularly because I was with them, and so he asked a group of young men to accompany us to the next village. Here the men handed us over to the village headman who instructed men from his village to accompany us to the next village, and so it went on till we reached what looked like a hermitage.

We stood at the gate and Ram called out, "Is anyone in?" and Rishi Valmiki appeared at the door. The Rishi's permanent hermitage was further north, he had taken his students on a pilgrimage and they had set up camp where we met them. We prostrated before the Rishi and Ram narrated to him the circumstances that had brought us here. I took an instant liking to the Rishi, he was so kind and wise, and he reminded me of my father. Years later I would meet him again. My husband asked the Rishi to direct us to a place where we may reside, a place where we would not disturb the hermits in meditation. Rishi Valmiki directed us to the hill at Chitrakoot, on the banks of the River Mandakini. He told us that after great penance Annasuya the wife of Rishi Attri had brought down the river for her husband.

This was the final lap of our journey; as we climbed the hill we saw herds of elephants and deer and a variety of birds wandering about completely unafraid of us, it was such a wonderful experience. We arrived at a clearing and Guha and Lakshman set about building a shelter, in no time at all they had built me a house! The Bhils accompanying us quickly made up a fire place over which I would cook and donated to us a few cooking utensils. Ram now asked Guha to return, with tears streaming down his eyes he bade us farewell; who knew that within a few weeks we would be seeing each other again.

As I lay in bed – a mat on the floor, that night I experienced a great sense of peace in the knowledge that we had arrived! This would be our home. It is strange how quickly one develops ownership, 'this is mine'; acquiring, accruing and then attaching - this is the thread of human life. What a paradox – the One who has created all this never even thinks of 'my or mine'; but all living beings have this sense of mine and theirs.

Life was showing me her various facets; today, Ram the son of the King of Kosala and Janaki the daughter of the Great Janak accepted with gratitude cooking pots from the villagers, when not a week back it was well within their means to provide cooking pots to the entire kingdom! Who is Ram? The one who would have been King of Kosala or the one who is gently snoring in the outer room? Who am

I? – Janak's daughter, the Queen of Kosala or this person sleeping on the mat? – and I drifted off into a deep sleep.

It was in Chitrakoot that I had the mind space to think of what Ram and Lakshman must have gone through during the last few days. What does one experience when one discovers that the object of one's hero worship has feet of clay; and if that person is a parent? I shuddered at the pain and anguish the brothers must experience but could not express.

Our life fell into a routine, Ram or Lakshman would go out for a walk in the morning and collect vegetables or wild beans for lunch. My experience in my mother's kitchenette served me well and I was able to feed my family! Lakshman often told me that I was the best cook in the world. I recall it as an idyllic period in my life. We would wander around the hillside, bathe in the river, hermits would come by and sit with us for a while. They were so happy that Ram and Lakshman were here on the hill to protect them from demons who wanted to destroy their peace. At other times Ram would narrate legends to Lakshman and me. As I wandered around the forest I was able to identify the medicinal herbs that Rishi Satananda's wife had told me about, I knew exactly which herb would be useful in a particular situation. In time even the hermits would consult me when they were ill. We were so happy I didn't miss Ayodhya at all, my husband was pleased at my ability to cope and that made me happiest. Chitrakoot was very quiet, the only sounds were the sounds of the birds in the day and the crickets and the animals at night; in fact the three of us had begun to speak in a low voice and I removed the bells on my anklets so as not to disturb the peace. My husband made me put the bells right back, he said he felt more at ease when he knew exactly where I was, Lakshman too thought it was a good idea to keep the bells on. The one thing I discovered about my husband's family was that they followed a very rigid code of conduct. Lakshman walked behind Ram, he ate only after Ram had begun eating and spoke only when Ram permitted him to and that signal was a faint twitch of the eyebrow – except the odd time as when he spoke to the Sage Parshuram and more recently to Sumantra. Lakshman never contradicted Ram. I wondered if Lakshman found this stifling; having grown up in a freer atmosphere in Mithila, sometimes I felt weighed down by these rules; of course at Chitrakoot I did not have to follow the rules because there was nobody other than us.

My husband was very romantic; he would string flowers for me to wear in my hair, on full moon nights we always took a long walk. He told me then how love struck he was when he saw me at the temple the day before the Swayamwar. That night he had compared my face to the full moon and felt I shone more brightly than the moon. I felt so pleased and good about him and myself.

One day early in the afternoon the three of us were sitting in the shade under a tree, when my husband suddenly frowned, "Lakshman do you hear the sounds, and see the dust rising in the north. I wonder what it is." Lakshman shinned up a tree and came down in a jiffy. He reported that he saw a large army coming towards Chitrakoot; the army carried the flag of Kosala. Clearly it was Bharat coming towards us with an army. Lakshman told Ram that they should now get ready for a battle. However, Ram said "My mind tells me that Bharat is here on a peaceful mission. I also know for sure that he had no hand in his mother's plan; so let us wait and see".

In a while we heard footsteps behind us; as we turned to look there appeared good friend Guha leading the way followed by Bharat, Shatrughna and Sumantra. Bharat and Shatrughna rushed up to Ram and fell at his feet and Ram picked them up and hugged them close. Bharat broke down, "I had no hand in this plan, please believe me", he managed to say as he choked over his tears. Ram consoled him like a father would console a child. "I have no doubt about that little one, but why are you crying? Do you doubt me, did you ever think I would have thought badly of you?" said Ram. That brought even more tears to Bharat's eyes; it was a while before Shatrughna got his share of affection; he was the baby of the family. Ram held him close and neither would let go. Sumantra discreetly stood aside. After this emotional reunion with Ram and Lakshman, Bharat and Shatrughna came and prostrated to me and Sumantra appeared on the scene. It was then that Sumantra told us about my father-in-law's passing on. I didn't know how to react; when I left, my father-in-law was in such a pitiable condition that I was not surprised at the news, but I felt so sorry that he had such a sad end; I did love him a lot. Ram's eyes filled with tears; he said, "Apart from the fact that I am going to miss him, knowing the grief he experienced in his last moments kills me".

Bharat and Shatrughna were followed by Rishi Vashistha, Mother Kaushalya, Mother Sumitra and Queen Kaikeyi. When I saw the mothers in austere clothing worn after a husband's passing on, I realised the import of my father-in-law's passing away. Mother Kaushalya and Sumitra hugged me and went in to inspect my little home, Queen Kaikeyi remained aloof I wondered why she had come at all.

So great was the people's love for Ram that almost half of Ayodhya had accompanied Bharat following the same arduous route we had taken. I was delighted to meet Arundhati the wife of Rishi Vashistha, Bhagirathi the wife of Sumantra and Shrutakirti, but wonder of wonders my father had come too! What joy that was, what comfort to be enveloped in his loving arms!

He told me that my mother and he had come to Ayodhya on hearing of King Dashrath's passing away and it was then they heard of our being sent off to live in the forest. Bharat had insisted that my father accompany him to meet Ram. His agreeing to come confirmed to Bharat that my father believed he had no role in this great drama. My mother had stayed behind in Ayodhya to spend time with Urmila. Father told me that Urmila had accepted the situation and although she was not grieving at the separation she was not her usual self and that caused him great sorrow. I felt so sorry for my little sister but there was nothing to be done, we must accept what fate has in store for us. If one moulds oneself according to the circumstances, just as Nature moulds herself according to the seasons, and follows the path of dharma, only then will one be happy.

A meeting of all the men was called; we ladies sat apart and watched the proceedings. Bharat had come to ask Ram to return, he was joined in his plea by all the others. He put this across to Ram, but my husband was not to be shaken from his path of Dharma. He said to Bharat, "One has to follow one's Dharma. Father gave his word, for him his word was greater than himself and I, as his son must help him keep his word. I brought Seeta with me because she told me it was a wife's Dharma to be with her husband. I am following my Dharma and ensuring another's Dharma is maintained. You too must follow Dharma and see that father's word is not falsified. As far as the people's desire is concerned, Dharma is not decided by numbers, and people's will and voice are fickle. Remember well, what the Raghu Race does, will be cited as classic norms by folks in all ages to come". Bharat was not convinced with Ram's arguments; he did not want the throne and said he would not be able to rule.

At this point they turned to my father, who also felt that Ram be allowed to follow his Dharma and Bharat take upon himself the duties of ruling the kingdom. Bharat reluctantly agreed but only after a promise from Ram that he would return after fourteen years and take over the Kingdom. Then Bharat asked Ram to step into a pair of sandals he had brought along for him; these, he said would be placed on the throne of Ayodhya. Bharat would rule in the name of Ram. I felt so sorry for the four brothers but especially for Bharat, his mother had let him down as well.

I had sometime alone with Shrutakirti; she told me that although Bharat had pleaded with Mandavi to come along she had remained behind. She had said she couldn't face me; she was so embarrassed, horrified and angry at what her mother-in-law had done. She had asked Shrutakirti to tell me repeatedly that neither she nor her husband had an inkling of what was going on in Queen Kaikeyi's head. I assured Shrutakirti that I had not an iota of doubt that Bharat and Mandavi were in no way involved and I still loved her as much.

Shrutakirti described to me how the four of them were greeted on their return from Bharat's grandfather's home. When they entered Kosala they saw a pall of gloom, the citizens greeted them but without a smile. They were nonplussed at this behaviour; usually people would rush out to greet the sons of their King. It was only when they reached the palace and discovered the truth did they understand. Bharat was livid with his mother and he no longer addressed her as 'mother', he referred to her as 'Her Highness.' As for Manthara, Shatrughna had kicked her in anger and knocked off her front teeth. Bharat had prevented any further onslaught and since then Manthara was never seen in public. Queen Kaikeyi too kept to herself.

It was now time for the Ayodhya party to leave; Ram was keen that they left as soon as possible because of the disturbance they may have caused to the meditating hermits. As they departed I saw Lakshman handing over a small bundle of fruits to his mother; needless to say they were for Urmila, I was touched by this gesture. It gave me the idea to send some back for Mandavi to assure her of my love.

When the party returned I was replaying the visit in my mind; Ram had said that he allowed me to accompany him because I told him it was my Dharma; I thought he allowed me to come because he loved me. This bothered me and I asked my husband at an opportune time; I was amazed at the answer. He said, "What I said holds good – I cannot live without you; but if your coming did not have the sanction of Dharma I would not have permitted you to come." I asked, "What about love?" Matter of fact, he replied, "My Dharma overrides every emotion and yours must too".

After the visit, life went on as usual; we spent our days in meditation or listening to legends of which Ram had an unending supply. We took long walks and would visit hermitages that dotted the hill sides. I was rarely left alone - either Ram or Lakshman would be there with me, whether in the hut or if I took a stroll.

We got news of Ayodhya from the people of Ayodhya who would come to visit Ram. Bharat was so distressed to have seen Ram and Lakshman living as ascetics; he decided he too would live the life of an ascetic; he ruled Ayodhya in Ram's name but lived in Nandigram a small village on the outskirts of Ayodhya. He dressed as an ascetic, slept on the floor and ate only fruit and tubers. Bharat had insisted that Mandavi continue to live in the palace and not with him in Nandigram. Although Shatrughna continued to live in the palace he too had taken the vow of celibacy. What had Queen Kaikeyi achieved? Her insistence of her boons being granted had resulted in three queens – Queens Kaushalya, Sumitra and herself losing their husband; and the married lives of four couples being disrupted. Of the four sisters perhaps I was the best off; at least I was not separated from my husband.

One day a group of hermits living on the hill came up to Ram to tell him they were leaving the hill. They said the demon Khara ruled this area, on the instructions of Ravana the demon King of Lanka, he had sent his men to disturb their meditation and desecrate their yagnas, so they had decided to move north. We were now alone and rather lonely on the hill, moreover the citizens of Ayodhya knew where we were and would often intrude on our privacy. My husband felt we had lived here long enough and it was time to move on; he decided we would move further south.

On the eve of our departure Ram gave me the Bala and Ati Bala Mantras given to him by Rishi Vishwamitra. The mantra gives strength and the power to endure hardships to one who practises it with devotion. It prevents hunger, thirst and physical fatigue and gives the person great spiritual strength. I told Ram about the yogic powers that Gargi had given me and he had said it explained my resilience, endurance and determination.

Our first halt in our journey south was Rishi Attri's hermitage. We were warmly welcomed by the Rishi and I had the opportunity to meet the Great Annasuya who I revered. Annasuya was known for her austerities and her benevolence. It was because of her prayers that the River Mandakini had come down from the heavens. As I bent down to touch her feet, she gathered me in her arms and sat me by her side. She then went into the inner room and brought out a saree that would always look new and fresh, and ornaments. I was hesitant at first to receive them but feared that my refusal may hurt Annasuya so I accepted these.

Annasuya said to me, "While I have given you ornaments, a woman's greatest ornament is her chastity. Motherhood is obvious but paternity is a matter of faith and trust. A single act of carelessness or waywardness could well destroy a lineage and so the great need for a woman to be chaste. Seeta your accompanying Ram will be lauded till the human race exists; you will be a role model as a wife and a mother. Fortitude, piety, friend and wife are put to test only in times of adversity; one who passes the trial in thought, word and deed is blessed; it is not by one's own effort but only with the grace of God that one may pass these trials, sometimes circumstances are so challenging that even the mighty fall, take the case of Ahalya, whom your husband redeemed".

I hadn't thought I had done anything extraordinary by accompanying my husband; as for being a role model for a mother, only the future would tell.

CHAPTER 8
Panchavati to Lanka

Rishi Attri had suggested that we set up base in the Dandaka[34] Forest, and so the next morning we set out towards the forest; it was dense and known to be inhabited by demons. As we walked into the forest we came across a variety of hermits, ascetics and hermitages. Some ascetics performed various types of severe austerities, we saw a bare bodied ascetic standing on one foot and another lay on a bed of nails. At one hermitage were a group of ascetics offering oblations to the fire; at yet another hermitage we saw the children of ascetics scampering around the hermitage.

I couldn't understand why some of these ascetics tortured their bodies. I was taught that our bodies are the temples where the spirit lives while we have a bodily experience, and that the body should be revered and respected. Was this the way of achieving dispassion and detachment and reaching knowledge or God? My father, Rishi Yaagnavalkya, Rishi Vashistha were realised Masters; they did not need to adopt

---

[34] North of the Vindhya Range of Mountains

these practices. My father was a householder and King, he enjoyed what life had given him and yet was detached and learned. Why my father? My own husband had given up his throne without a hint of remorse; had he wanted to put up a fight to claim his right, all of Ayodhya would have stood by him. When I brought this up with my husband, he said, "Attachment and passion is the root cause of sorrow, if one is free from within, attachment and detachment are of no consequence"[35]; and we continued walking.

When we reached the hermitage suggested by Rishi Attri, the hermits welcomed us and offered us shelter. They told Ram that the demons in the forest had made life unbearable for them; since as hermits they had no weapons for self defence, the demons were a law unto themselves. Ram asked them to be unafraid and assured them that he and Lakshman would render the forest safe for them. We spent the night at the hermitage and the next morning set out again. A while into the forest a huge grotesque apparition appeared in front of us, "Viradha is my name and I want her as my wife," he bellowed, and grabbed me. At first Ram was transfixed and then he burst into tears; Lakshman prodded him and then both attacked and killed this creature. Later Ram said to me, "I was so terrified that the demon would harm you, I lost my nerve". This was my first face to face encounter with the demons, but it would not be my last.

We continued walking through the forest stopping at hermitages in our path including Rishi Sarbhanga's

---

[35]   Unpublished talks of Sadguru K Sivananda Murthy

hermitage. We were welcomed and made comfortable everywhere. Ram was particularly keen to seek the blessings of Rishi Agastya but we had not yet come upon his hermitage. When we halted at Rishi Sutikshna's hermitage Ram asked for directions. Rishi Sutikshna was a disciple of Rishi Agastya and was very keen to meet him, but, as a disciple he could not go to his teacher unless summoned, for Rishi Sutikshna this was a golden opportunity and so Rishi Sutikshna accompanied us to Rishi Agastya's hermitage.

Rishi Agastya was performing a yagna along with other Rishis of the area, when we arrived. Rishi Sutikshna went ahead and announced our arrival to Rishi Agastya. The teacher, far from chastising his disciple for arriving without being summoned, blessed him for leading Ram to his hermitage. He got up from the yagna, came and hugged Ram and Lakshman and blessed me. I then went in search of Lopamudra, his wife. Lopamudra was the daughter of the King of Vidharba; she was learned and wise. She welcomed me with open arms; I did not need to tell her the circumstances of my appearing at her doorstep. She sat me down, offered me some fruits and we talked like old friends. She said, "I admire you Seeta, for leaving the comfort of the palace to be with your husband; perhaps you are blessed that you don't fear the unknown". I replied, "Mother, I admire you a hundred times more. You were born a princess, yet you married a Sage and agreed to live in the forest forever; I will return to Ayodhya in a couple of years. Of course a very different Seeta will return to Ayodhya, I have seen life from various angles now. I have experienced malice and cunning; kindness and devotion. Nothing will surprise me any longer;

except for God we all have feet of clay. I leave it to God to keep me on the path of Dharma."

"Seeta! Go forth without fear, the divinity within you will guide you and come to your assistance at every crossroad; the world will admire you not only for your loyalty to your husband, but for your sense of duty towards your children and thereby for doing your duty to the throne of Kosala".

Children! I had not even thought of the prospect.

On Rishi Agastya's advice, we moved further into the forest and came upon a clearing encircled by five banyan trees. The place was perfect to build a hut. Lakshman got down to it straightaway and we had a perfect little hut. Unused to human beings, the birds were unafraid and would perch on my shoulder and peck out of my hand. Soon a huge vulture made his appearance; although I couldn't provide him a full meal, he would come down and eat the tidbits I offered him. He took it upon himself to guard the hut, he wouldn't mind the birds and the squirrels but he hissed and darted at the rats and snakes around the hut. His very presence kept away wild dogs and jackals; we named him Jatayu – or a bird with divine qualities. He spent his day in the skies or in the jungles hunting for his prey, but no sooner did any outsider come near the hut I would see him watching us perched on a branch of a tree close by.

One afternoon we sat in the shade of the banyan trees listening to the chirping of the birds. Looking towards Jatayu relish some raw flesh off a carcass, Ram said, "The same life exists in the same way in a million species. Yet, each species functions differently as a rule. Likewise, there are different grades even among the same species, say human beings for example, though 'life' is one and the same in all of them. We have seen that the similarities or commonalties do not help; neither do differences. All of us are here, stuck in various degrees, only to find a way out. Each one is working his destiny in his own way"[36].

Suddenly we heard a noise in the bushes and a woman stepped out, she was tall and dark, she had a huge nose and huge ears, she looked deformed. Then this apparition smiled, baring her large teeth and red gums, the sight was frightening. She came up to Ram and said, "I have been watching you for some days, I have taken a liking to you, marry me". My imperturbable husband looked toward me and said, "She is my wife". I kept my eyes averted I couldn't even look up at the creature. She then turned to Lakshman, who pointing to Ram said, "I am his servant, he who is the King of Kosala, the son of King Dashrath". Thereupon the brazen woman addressed Ram, "He is your servant, I have no use for him, I want you, cast aside this weakling and I will give you joy." She then ran up to where we were sitting and grabbed my hair, even before I could scream, she let loose her grasp and began howling. When I looked up there were drops of blood on the ground and she had fled. Lakshman had attacked her. I was trembling like a leaf, Ram held me close and we went into the hut. Ram told us she was Surpanakha, the younger sister of Ravana the King of Lanka. He then cautioned us, "This is not the

---

[36] Unpublished talks of Sadguru K Sivananda Murthy

end, more will follow, be alert. We have invited the wrath of Ravana, but it will give us an opportunity to put an end to his tyranny in the forest and in Lanka".

I felt bad that my husband had to take up this fight to protect me; when I mentioned this to him, he said, "Seeta, you are the love of my life, for you I will fight the world". Then winking at me, he said, "It happens to be my Dharma!"

The next morning Ram saw a group of demons led by Surpanakha walking towards the hut. He asked me to go into a cave near the hut and Lakshman to stand on guard at the entrance of the cave. I pleaded with Lakshman to go and assist Ram, but he assured me that Ram alone was equal to double their number. Ram strung his bow and within minutes it was all over; he had managed to kill them all. When he returned he told us they were Khara's men and now we should be prepared for another round of fighting.

Khara sent an emissary with a message that Ram should hand me over to them and he and Lakshman should leave the forest. Ram replied that they were Kshatriyas and ready for a battle. If Khara's people did not have the strength to fight they should retreat. No Kshatriya worth his name would attack a retreating army. A larger army of the demons followed; Ram sent me back to the cave with Lakshman guarding me and Ram took on the army alone. A frightful battle ensued at the end of which, Khara and his two brothers Trishira and Dushan were killed. The hermits living in the forest came to thank Ram for ridding the forest of evil, but for some reason, Lakshman was not at ease.

One morning when I stepped out to fetch flowers to offer at my altar, I spied a beautiful golden bejewelled deer gambolling in the thicket near the hut. I was captivated, and called out to Ram and Lakshman to have a look. I begged Ram to capture the deer for me. Lakshman stood by, sceptical. "This is Mareech in disguise", he said.

Lakshman explained that Mareech was the maternal uncle of Ravana, his mother Tadaka had been killed by Ram when they were with Rishi Vishwamitra. Around the same time Ram had fought the two other demons Subahu and Mareech. While Subahu had been killed, Mareech had been thrown miles away with the force of Ram's arrow.

Nevertheless Ram decided to go out and capture the deer for me. Lakshman was to stay behind and wait till Ram returned. Ram was away for a long time and then we heard Ram's voice call out Lakshman! Seeta! I panicked, I was sure Ram was in trouble; but Lakshman was not moved, again he said this is Mareech up to his tricks. Ram is invincible in a fight and he certainly would not cry for help. This time I was not convinced, I begged Lakshman to go. Lakshman refused saying Ram had asked him to stay and so he would stay. The calls for help became more frequent and were becoming fainter as if Ram was moving further away. I was in a state of complete panic and fear, I again pleaded with Lakshman, who now would not even respond to my pleas. When I heard Ram again, I could just not take it any longer, I said many harsh words to Lakshman; he ignored my pleas, but then I said "Lakshman you are not going because you are tired of your celibate status and if Ram is killed the coast will be clear for you". Lakshman turned ashen and coldly said "I am going, but make sure you do not step out of the hut".

The moment these words were out of my mouth, I regretted them, but once an arrow leaves the quiver and words roll off the tongue, there is no return. How often Ram had said, "A person should be in control of one's emotions, if emotions take control, all is lost". I had thought that he was making a reference to his father; I realised now it applied to each one of us.

Only a few weeks earlier I had said to Lopamudra, "Nothing will surprise me any more" but then I had not thought of myself, I had thought I was 'perfection incarnate' I could never have believed that I would lose control over my mind and emotions and my Dharma – I considered Lakshman a son, and what had I accused him of! I too had feet of clay!

I had failed! I had failed myself – no other. Janaki the daughter of Janak had no control over her emotions or her tongue – what would my husband say if he were to hear what I said; what would my father have said? I was mortified at the thought.

When Lakshman left, I wondered if it was the right thing to have sent him; also I was ashamed of what I said but it was too late now to call him back. I sat down at my altar and asked Mother Parvati to forgive me. Just then I heard a hermit call for alms; this I thought was a sign that I had done the right thing in sending Lakshman, and, that I was forgiven. I collected a few fruits and took them out to the hermit. I was concentrating on putting the fruits into the hermit's bag which he had put down on the ground when he suddenly swooped on me, picked me up, and started running. I couldn't even scream - I was so shocked!

He ran with me a little distance into the forest and there hidden in the foliage was his chariot. He dumped me into the chariot, and threw off his disguise. I was shocked at the ugliness of the man. "I am Surpanakha's brother", he said; that's when I discovered this was Ravana, the Demon King of Lanka! Suddenly the chariot rose above the trees and I screamed, I was terrified. Ravana said, "Don't be scared, I won't harm you. This chariot is a mechanical bird that travels in the air and is known as Pushpak, it belonged to Kubera[37] but I thought I could put it to better use".

He continued, "You are more beautiful than what Surpanakha described to me. I will make you my wife. You will have all the comforts you dream of; I can assure you it will be a better life than a life in the forest".

I suddenly found my voice and began screaming Ram! Ram! Who could have heard me scream so far above the ground? But someone did, good old Jatayu! He appeared from nowhere and swooped down on that airborne chariot, but he was no match for the King of Lanka who struck him with a sword. Blood dripping from his chest, Jatayu tried hard to bring down the Pushpak, but then I saw him fall through the air - one of his wings had been cut off by Ravana. My only saviour had fallen.

---

[37] The God of Wealth

I continued screaming but to no avail, thoughts rushed through my mind, how would Ram know had happened? Would he find Jatayu? How would he know where to look for me? So I began throwing my ornaments in the hope that they would lead Ram to wherever this demon was taking me. I threw away every ornament, everything except the necklace Ram had given me on his birthday, I couldn't part with it.

I told him to turn the chariot around, "Do you realise I am the wife of Ram the King of Kosala; and you have the nerve to ask me to be your wife? Turn around now, else when my husband discovers you have abducted me he will attack you, he has already destroyed your army. Now do you want to be destroyed your self?" I said. The ogre replied, "If your husband is that great what is he doing wandering about in the forest with his wife in tow; why didn't he claim his right?" I realised that there was no point in engaging with this man, I prayed to Mother Parvati and asked her to protect me. Fear and guilt were suffocating me. Fear of what this man would do to me; I had heard from childhood that 'I' was not the body and the body was an impermanent temple to house my spirit; nevertheless the fear was for my life and for violation of my body. Guilt consumed me; I couldn't forgive myself for what I had said to Lakshman.

We continued travelling over clouds in the chariot and Ravana continued talking about what marriage to him would mean for me. The thought of anybody other than Ram as my husband was unthinkable in the first place and then to have to hear Ravana expressing his desire to marry me was positively revolting. "You can have whatever you desire; every comfort you can dream of, you'll be waited upon hand and foot by thousands of maids. You will be my chief queen", he rambled on. When he said you will be my chief queen, I thought of Queen Kaikeyi, who was the architect of this situation. I had decided to keep silent and silent I was, as the chariot came down on the ground. Ravana's courtiers rushed to greet him; one look at them and I lowered my eyes, I couldn't bear the sight. Each one was more ugly, hideous and revolting than the other.

I recall going up a long staircase with Ravana babbling about the beauty of his palace. He took me on a tour of the palace, I took in very little and remembered even less, but I do remember him pointing out the gilded pillars, another time he pointed out to the gems inlaid on the walls. I think I found the palace dazzling, but was never sure if it was my state of mind or the palace that dazzled me. I was later told that the palace had been built by the celestial architect Vishwakarma for Kubera and Ravana had usurped it from Kubera. The palace was very large, that I remember well, and after a long tour Ravana took me to a chamber. A couple of unsightly and repulsive demonesses were awaiting us, at least they were women and would be kind, or so I thought, how wrong I was! They banged down a plate of food in front of me; I was not hungry and pushed the plate away. Howling with laughter they went to tell their King about my refusal to eat. Ravana stomped in and warned me, that this behaviour would not be tolerated and I had to accept that this was now my home.

Although I was trembling with fear I told Ravana, "You call yourself the King of Lanka, but you are worse than a jackal; a jackal slinks around, but without disguise, to eat the remains of a carcass; but you wicked creature, you disguised yourself as a hermit and abducted a helpless lady. Why didn't you fight my husband one on one, you coward? You may have survived after abducting the wife of Indra, but by abducting me, the wife of Ram, you are doomed. You may kill me if you want but no self respecting woman will agree to your request".

Ravana roared in anger, "Her husband is a spineless creature roaming the forests, and she is as foolish as she is beautiful. Does she really think her husband can challenge me? Take her away to the Ashoka Van[38] and bring her down to her knees, but don't destroy her beauty." Turning to face me he said, "Woman, I am giving you a few weeks to appreciate your good fortune, at the end of which if you don't agree to marry me, you may consider it your last day on earth", and with that he stomped off.

---

[38] Grove of Ashoka Trees

CHAPTER 9
A Year in Lanka

The demoness in charge of me then led me out of the palace and we walked some distance and entered a grove of fruit trees. I could smell the fruit, the fragrant flowers and despite the presence of the huge demons guarding the trees, the place was peaceful. We arrived at an unused temple complex and entered a cottage at the end of the grove. I had hoped this would be my home, only for a few days, but it would be almost a year before I left the cottage. The ogresses kept me company, their main task was to beat me into submission; they would howl and scream all the while singing praises of Ravana, I would not react and this infuriated them. Without exception they were all deformed. When I looked at them I remembered my childhood nightmare of being among strange people. Tryakshi was the demoness with three eyes; Ekapada had only one leg and Eklochana had only one eye. I pitied these 'women' fate had been cruel to them and they knew no better than to wail and howl. I was so grateful to the Sage Gargi for initiating me into yogic practices and my husband for having initiated me into the mantras of Bala and Ati Bala - they helped me maintain my sanity.

At sunset my guards would depart and leave me to myself. I looked forward to the peace at that time. I often thought of my life in Mithila, how safe and secure my childhood had been. Marriage sure was a package deal! I had once thought that in the given situation I was the best off amongst us four sisters, not any more. They were safe at home and I was at the mercy of a demon king. I wondered if my parents knew that I had been abducted and with a jolt I would be back in the present. Days turned to weeks and weeks to months. This was the thirteenth year we were away from Ayodhya and at the end of the year we should have been returning to Ayodhya, but how was I to get out of here? They were too many guards, and we had crossed a large water body, when we were returning to Ayodhya on the very same Pushpak that brought me to Lanka, Ram told me it was an ocean. Even if I were to escape where would I find Ram? I missed Ram a lot, Ram was the only word on my lips. I had a lot of time for introspection; my rational mind told me that what I said to Lakshman was indefensible but that did not give Ravana the licence to abduct me. I came to the conclusion that I could be censured for my vitriolic attack on Lakshman but I could not be faulted if I was abducted. If a thief breaks into a home is the thief at fault for breaking into the house or the owner for having a house?

One day Mandodari, the wife of Ravana came to plead with me to accept his proposal. She said that there was no escape from Lanka and I should make peace with my situation. No woman had ever rejected his overtures and because of my rejection Ravana was in a foul mood and vented his anger on poor Mandodari. Life was so unbearable for Mandodari that she swallowed her pride and spoke to me. It must have been extremely painful for Mandodari to come to me, another woman, and ask me to respond to her husband's advances. I heard her out and decided not to respond, there was no way that I was going to either live here for the rest of my life or even contemplate Ravana's proposal – I was a married woman and very much in love with my husband.

Some months into my stay in the Ashoka Van, a new attendant joined the rest. She looked more human than the others, her name was Trijata. When we had a moment together she told me that Ravana was the older brother of her father Vibhishan, and she had used that connection to be appointed as an attendant. Trijata was sympathetic to my ordeal but couldn't help much, except by being kind. She told me that although they were related, her family did not approve of Ravana's behaviour but in fact admired Ram. She assured me that Ram would come and rescue me and that I should have patience. Vibhishan, his wife Sarama and his two daughters Anala and Trijata were devotees of Vishnu, like my mother – but at that instant it did not help much, to learn about this.

Trijata told me that Ravana's father was Vishrava and his mother Kaikesi. I could not help notice the similarity in the names 'Kaikesi' and 'Kaikeyi'! Trijata went on to tell me that Ravana had two brothers, Kumbhakaran and her father Vibhishan; and one sister Surpanakha. Ravana was a great devotee of Lord Shiva; he had constructed over 700,000 temples for Shiva in Lanka, but would not permit the worship of Vishnu[39]. Ravana had meditated for many years and appealed to Shiva. Shiva was pleased with him and had granted him great strength. Shiva had also given him a sword called the Chandrahaas with a caveat that should Ravana ever use it against the dictates of Dharma the sword would return to Shiva and Ravana would be destroyed.

Trijata told me that Ravana was not only very powerful but also hot tempered; nobody in the court dared to differ with him, because their life was at stake. Yet most of his ministers had disapproved of Ravana's abducting me and were counselling him to send me back to wherever Ram could be found, but Ravana would not relent.

One evening I was particularly depressed; there was no sign that I was ever going to leave Lanka. Just then Ravana arrived at the Ashoka Van along with Mandodari and his other wives. He strode ahead and the wives were cowering behind him.

"Beautiful maiden it is now eleven months that you are here, at least now accept me as your husband, Mandodari and all my wives will serve you. I will make you happier than you have

---

[39] Brahma, Vishnu and Shiva form the Hindu Trinity representing, basic life cycle of creation, existence and destruction. Brahma is associated with creation or the beginning, Vishnu is associated with life and existence and Shiva is associated with bringing to an end all creation. The Trinity represents three aspects of the one God.

ever been in your life. Remember that with each passing day, your youth passes too and this will not return. Make the best use of the body God has endowed you with". I was furious but I kept my cool and allowed him to go on. "Are you still waiting for that Ram wearing tattered clothes and roaming the forest? I wonder if he is still alive. In any case he is inferior to me in strength, in wealth and in fame", he continued.

Holding a blade of grass to indicate a wall between Ravana and me I said. "Turn your mind away from another's wife, Oh King! And take care of your own wives. Your wealth does not tempt me; neither do your glories impress me – that is if you have any. When you compare yourself to Ram, you expose your ignorance and arrogance. Compared to Ram, you are like a fire fly and he, the sun. The Lord of Death may spare you but my enraged husband Ram and my brother-in-law Lakshman will crush you like an ant. In your own interest, let me go".

Ravana stood speechless on hearing what I had to say. Then he rushed towards me with his sword raised, at the same instant Mandodari rushed and stood in front of me preventing him from attacking me. He left in a rage saying to me "You have one month to make up your mind, else your neck will meet this sword – this is the Chandrahaas." Turning to the demonesses he said, "It is your task to beat her into submission."

I wished Ravana had killed me there and then; one month was too long to wait. The demonesses started howling and screaming and dancing around me, Trijata who was in-charge of them silenced them and said, "Listen! I had a dream the other night, a monkey came from across the ocean and burnt our Lanka. I saw our King, naked on a donkey going toward the south, the Loka of the ancestors". Hearing this, the demonesses stopped their cacophony, fell at my feet, apologised and left.

I then told Trijata to get me some fire and wood so that I may immolate myself, I couldn't take this torture any longer. Again Trijata said to me, "Have patience, Ram will come", but she too left. I was all alone and the tears that I had been holding back now flowed freely, I wept for what seemed an age.

There was not a sound in the Ashoka Van, even the crickets seemed to sense my despondency and were silent. In this silence I heard something fall near me, it was a hard metallic sound; I was distracted, I looked around and saw a ring on the floor of the hut. I picked it up and was sure I was hallucinating; it was Ram's signet ring! As I was wondering if I was dead or alive, normal or hallucinating, I heard a sweet voice sing Ram's glories. I made sure that I was awake and in my senses and called out into the night, "Whoever sings these glories show yourself to me". There was a thud and a little monkey landed near me. I was dismayed and frightened, but the monkey spoke to me – in those days, animals and birds could speak the language of humans. He said, "Fear not Mother, I am the one who dropped the ring, I am Hanuman a servant of the great Ram. I have been sent to search for you and Ram sent his ring so that you don't despair. Mother, Ram will come; have patience."

'Have patience'! I could have screamed in despair hearing those words. I swallowed hard and then asked Hanuman, "How is my husband? Does he ever think of me? Why hasn't he come so far?

Hanuman answered, "Your husband, Lord Ram and his brother Lakshman are physically fine, but dejected and sad without you - Lord Ram particularly, although he doesn't say much, his desperation to find you indicates his unhappiness and sorrow. The brothers have been searching the forests all these months and on specific information that you are in Lanka I have been sent to locate you. My Lord Ram has sent a message for you, he asked me to tell you that life was not worth living without you. He has nobody to talk to; no shoulder to cry on, he is so unhappy that rain drops which normally cool a person, sear his skin".

"Mother, do not be anxious any longer; no sooner I go back, Lord Ram will arrive here with an army."

"Now I must hurry back, but I am hungry; as I entered the garden I saw trees laden with fruit. If you permit me, I'll have some fruit and then take something from you as a sign that I have met you and return to where Lord Ram is waiting for news".

I was happy to allow this monkey Hanuman to eat the fruit, but warned him that huge demons guard the trees; he was unperturbed and scampered off. He returned after a long while all covered with soot and wet. "What happened to you? Why did you take so long, why are you black all over and why are you wet?" I shot off a volley of questions.

"When I was eating the fruit, Meghnad the son of King Ravana caught hold of me, tied me up and took me to Ravana's court. I tried to convince the King that he should ensure safe passage to you to return to your husband but the evil man laughed me off. There was great commotion in the court about what they would do to me. You see, Mother, in the scuffle I killed a couple of demons and one of them was Ravana's son Aksha Kumar. Ravana naturally wanted to punish me; killing me would be unethical since I was an emissary of another King, so they swathed my tail with cloth dipped in oil and lit it. No sooner had they set my tail on fire, than I escaped and ran around the city, everything that came in contact with my tail caught fire. I then jumped into the sea to put out the fire and now here I am! You know Mother the entire city is burning - but I must leave now, Lord Ram is waiting for me. Mother please give me something to show my Lord that I have met you and what message should I take to him from you?" I took off the necklace Ram had given me and handed it to Hanuman saying, "Tell your Lord Ram that if he doesn't come within a month he won't see me alive. Tell him to hurry - I cannot bear it any longer." Hanuman assured me that Ram would come soon, and then bounded away.

That night I slept in peace after months, I was so relieved that my husband and Lakshman were well and that my husband had not forgotten me. The next morning the disconsolate Seeta of the last eleven months woke up with hope. "My Ram is coming!" I said to myself and hugged myself. I thought my emotions were dead, but no, Ram coming for me, brought back all my emotions of love and hope. That morning I thought the chirping of the birds was particularly sweet and as the sun rose the fragrance of flowers wafted into my cottage and I smiled to myself. The first smile in months! Soon the demonesses returned, this time wailing and sobbing that their homes were burnt to ashes. So far I had felt sorry for myself, today there was hope in my heart and I felt good enough about myself to feel for them. I was sorry for them, their homes had been burnt, but I did not feel guilty that my husband's emissary was the cause of their sorrow; their King was the root cause of their sorrow.

"Trijata, part of your dream has manifested itself, so the other will also manifest", they wailed. They described Hanuman as a monkey the size of a mountain with four arms and a magical tail. That day onward the demonesses changed their attitude towards me and I, towards them; they went all out to please me and because of my new found hope I felt charitable towards them. I realised one can feel good about others only when one feels good about one's own self.

One morning Trijata came looking under the weather, she told me that in the court, her father Vibhishan and a few others were counselling Ravana not to be stubborn and ensure me safe passage to Ram, they told Ravana that he was bringing about his down fall. Vibhishan had said to Ravana - that lust, anger, vanity and covetousness were the paths that led to one's destruction; as King, Ravana's conduct had to be exemplary; he had urged Ravana to follow the path of righteousness and protect his people. So infuriated was Ravana with this advice that he had kicked Vibhishan and asked him to take refuge with Ram whose virtues he was so vociferously advocating. Her father had then actually sought protection from Ram. I regarded this a good omen.

I was wondering where Ram would collect an army to fight Ravana. Although Hanuman had told me that he and other monkeys would be fighting on Ram's side, I was sceptical about their being able to fight the mighty demons. I brushed aside my scepticism and told myself that God had brought me this far, he would take care of the rest. That I would be reunited with my beloved, I had no doubt.

Trijata told me that after the 'monkey episode' people were frightened and feared that the burning of Lanka was only the beginning of their misfortune. One day she reported that Ram and his army, comprising of monkeys, had crossed the ocean and landed in Lanka. My patience and despair turned to impatience and hope. I couldn't wait to see my Ram. Ram and Ravana were now officially at war, the battle raged on for nine days.

On the tenth day, which was the tenth day of the bright fortnight of the month of Ashwin[40], Trijata was very depressed but couldn't find the reason for her misery; she said she felt misfortune in her bones, she sensed something terrible was in store. That evening, just after sunset, her sister Anala came with the news that Ravana had been killed by Ram. Trijata started sobbing, "I knew my brother would come to this end, the law of Karma never fails, but he was

---

[40] corresponding to October –November of the Georgian Calendar

my brother," she sobbed. I felt sorry for the sisters although for me it was cause for celebration. My thoughts then turned to Mandodari, I was told she had entreated Ravana not to be stubborn and return me to Lord Ram but he had scoffed at her. I would never forget how she had prevented Ravana from attacking me on his last visit. Poor lady, however rash and arrogant Ravana was, he was her husband, and what had she done to deserve this.

The next morning while I was sitting in the cottage waiting for word from Ram, Hanuman dropped down from a tree. This time I was not scared and welcomed him. "Mother the war is over and Lord Ram has sent a message that he awaits you", he said. My heart leapt with joy; finally I would be reunited with my beloved Ram.

In a while the new king of Lanka, King Vibhishan and his wife Queen Sarama came to take me to the palace. "We are here to take you to the palace to have you dressed to be presented to Lord Ram. On behalf of the people of Lanka, we beg forgiveness for your trials and tribulations", said Queen Sarama. The thought that this was the Queen of Lanka speaking to the Queen of Kosala crossed my mind.

"I'd rather Ram see me as I am", I said.

Sarama said, "If the world sees you like this, they will say that Vibhishan is no different from his brother. For our sake, please dress as you would in Ayodhya".

We spend much of our lives living according to the expectations of others; and so I allowed myself to be taken to what was now Vibhishan's palace. At the palace I dressed to meet Ram, I felt just the way I did on the morning of the Swayamwar- there were butterflies in my stomach and I was nervous. Queen Sarama brought vermilion to adorn my parting. Hanuman who witnessed this asked me why I was wearing vermillion; I told him that this was my way of expressing joy at meeting Ram, and also a prayer that he may have a long life. He snatched the vermillion from a startled Queen Sarama and emptied the contents over his head and then proceeded to cover his entire body with the vermillion powder. When asked what he was doing, he said his joy at seeing his Lord Ram was so great that he needed to express it on his whole body, never mind that he must have seen Ram only an hour earlier; and the more vermillion he put on himself the longer Ram would live.

When Ram discovered the reason why Hanuman covered himself in vermilion, he was touched. He is reported to have said, "Hanuman whoever offers you vermillion will be able to overcome all hurdles in life and have a long life".

I stepped into the palanquin and we set out in a procession to the place where Ram was waiting for me; it reminded me of my wedding day, but how much water had flowed under the bridge. This was not that Seeta, neither was this that Ram; we had been through much and how this separation would have changed him and 'us' was yet to be seen.

The palanquins came to a halt in a courtyard and as I stepped down, Lakshman came and prostrated to me. I held him close, "I'm sorry my son, please forgive me", I said through a veil of happy tears. "We are together now and that is all that matters", he said smiling at me. How thin and dark he had become, my Lakshman! Then Lakshman led me up a few steps and stopped. I raised my head and looked straight into the black eyes of my beloved Ram. The same wave of excitement passed through me as when I had first seen him on the eve of the Swayamwar at the Shiva Parvati temple. I joined my hands in greeting and looked down, I couldn't bear to look at him in public, I didn't trust my emotions.

Then the King of Ayodhya addressed me in a voice that reached everybody, "How can I the scion of Raghus accept you since you have lived in another man's home? What example is this that I set for my people to live by?" I calmly turned to Lakshman and said, "Son, please light a fire. If I am pure I will come through unscathed, else I will meet my just end". Lakshman was horrified; he just stood rooted to the spot and there was pin drop silence in the crowd. Ram was aware that I had the yogic power to walk over hot coals; and never doubted my loyalty to him; but as King, he had to set an example to his people. He was now following the Dharma of a King, he had to lead and he would lead from the front, his people would follow his example. "Lakshman, do as she says", said the King of Kosala.

The coals were glowing and red hot; I halted a moment and prayed to the Fire God Agni and to Mother Parvati to be with me. I could never recall the experience, one moment I was standing in front of red hot coals, with Ram and a stricken Lakshman behind me and the next instant I had walked over the coals unscathed and Ram was in front of me. As I stepped out I had a clear vision of Ram and I being husband and wife in many earlier lives.

Ram loudly declared to the people "I bless each one of you, may you be as pure as your Queen Seeta and my beloved wife". The one who clapped and cheered the loudest was my dear Hanuman all covered in vermillion. At the first opportunity Ram apologized for making me go through the ordeal, "Seeta, I never ever doubted you; neither you nor I have a thought for another and we both know that. You know well that walking over fire is a yogic feat that requires great concentration; and even the slightest distraction means failure. That level of concentration is only possible for a person with a strong mind; and the characteristic of a strong mind is one who does not waver from the path of Dharma. The ability to walk over hot coals indicates strength of character which may be interpreted to mean purity. Seeta, it was not your husband who said those words; it was the King of Kosala. Never forget that what the Raghu Race does will be cited as classic norms by folks in all ages to come".

It occurred to me then that one classic norm would be that a woman would always have to prove her chastity; but should it not be her fault, would she still be faulted? As a loud yes resounded in my head, I saw hundreds of women in the past, present and future - used, abused, violated and then judged by society. The innocent man would never be wrong; his actions would always arise because the woman enticed him. Poor Man! How powerless he is off the battle field!

Ram then sent Hanuman off to Ayodhya to ascertain if Bharat was still waiting for Ram's return. If Bharat was indeed waiting for Ram to be crowned King of Ayodhya, Hanuman was to tell him that we were on our way back. Otherwise Hanuman was not to say anything but just come back and Ram would decide the next course of action.

Hanuman returned the next day to tell Ram that Bharat was eagerly waiting for Ram and had he not got the news that Ram was on his way to Ayodhya, he would have immolated himself.

Vibhishan was very keen that we spend a few days in Lanka. He told Ram, that he wanted me to go back to Ayodhya with pleasant memories of Lanka; but we were eager and impatient to return to Ayodhya, we had our share of adventures for more than one life time. Ram wanted to go back to his mothers; Bharat was also waiting for him. Vibhishan then arranged for the Pushpak to be readied for the return journey. The very Pushpak that had brought me to Lanka was now ready to take us back to Ayodhya. Vibhishan looked so mournful at our leaving, that Ram asked him to accompany us to Ayodhya; needless to say, Hanuman was with us.

We flew over the city of Lanka which was still grand despite the fire caused by Hanuman and the war. Ram pointed out the ocean that one had to cross to reach Lanka. We had all come to Lanka in different ways; I had flown in the Pushpak over the ocean, Hanuman had leapt over the ocean and Ram and his army had come over a bridge they themselves had constructed. Ram told me that it took his army of monkeys and squirrels five days to build the bridge.

"Squirrels?" I asked.

Ram smiled, "Yes squirrels; they scurried back and forth from the seashore to the bridge, carrying small pebbles in their mouths. They dropped the pebbles wherever they found space between the big rocks brought by the monkeys. These pebbles were very necessary to keep the rocks in place. It is the small things that make the big difference."

When Ram stroked them in gratitude, three white stripes appeared on the back of the little grey squirrels, to remind posterity that they too had helped Ram build the bridge.

Ram told me how shocked he was, when he returned after killing the deer to find the cottage empty. Ram had no intention of killing the deer, he just wanted to capture the deer and bring it back for me. But during the chase the deer led Ram further and further away from our hut; and then began shrieking "Lakshman! Seeta!" That's when Ram strung his bow to capture the animal. As Ram's arrow pierced the deer; the deer shrieked, Lakshman! Seeta! for the last time and dropped dead. Ram realised that the shrieking spelt danger and so he left the deer where it was and turned back. On the way he met Lakshman. Both hurried back to the cottage expecting misfortune and it stared them in the face.

Ram broke down in grief running hither and thither looking for me; subsequently they met the injured Jatayu who lay bleeding on the ground waiting for Ram. Once he told Ram that he saw me being taken to the south, he departed from his body.

We flew over a small cottage and Ram told me that this was the home of one Shabari who belonged to the Bhil tribe. Shabari was married off when she was very young. After the wedding was solemnised, her husband saw her face for the first time. Shabari was not the best looking of girls and her husband decided that he did not want her as his wife so left her in the forest. The little girl reached the hermitage of Rishi Matang who took care of the child. The Rishi gave her the 'Ram' mantra; when she asked the Rishi what it meant the Rishi told her, "You chant the name of 'Ram' and he will come to you one day". That day onwards Shabari chanted the mantra and waited for 'Ram'. Every morning she swept her little courtyard and plucked seasonal wild berries to offer Ram. Years passed, Shabari grew old and bent but she didn't give up hope. Rishi Matang left his mortal coil but Shabari's routine continued; her Guru had said that Ram would come and so she waited but not in vain. One day when Shabari had as usual swept her courtyard and had 'Ber' Shiva's favourite fruit ready to offer Ram two ascetics came to her cottage – Ram and Lakshman. Her mission in life was accomplished, Ram had come to her cottage and she was blessed. Ram had tears in his eyes as he recalled the affection with which she offered him fruit. Ram would often narrate this story and every time his eyes would be moist with tenderness.

Back in Ayodhya Ram made arrangements for Shabari to be taken care of. I asked Ram what he thought of Shabari's husband's conduct. Ram had replied, "I am not a judge, but men who do not respect and protect mothers, sisters and daughters have no place in the Kingdom of Kosala".

After crossing Shabari's cottage we reached Rishi Bharadwaj's hermitage, he had been following our movements and was aware of the Lanka experience. This time Ram did not stand at the gate, the hum of the Pushpak brought the Rishi out into the garden; he stood there welcoming us back. Our Vanvas started here and it was only proper for us to end it here with the Rishi's blessings.

I was keen that we retrace our steps to thank God for bringing us back safe. On the banks of the River Ganga, we offered flowers to the mighty river and collected the Ganga Water to take back to Ayodhya. Kevat was waiting for us in his boat and now accepted his payment. Ram pointed out Rishi Valmiki's hermitage as we flew over the confluence of the River Ganga and the Tamsa. When we reached Sringverpur, our Pushpak touched down in Guha's village. Guha was delighted to see us and now we could visit his home. Ram invited Guha to Ayodhya on the condition that he would return to his home as early as possible.

As the Pushpak flew into Ayodhya I recognised all the landmarks; it was as if I had left Ayodhya the day before and not fourteen years ago!

CHAPTER 10
Ayodhya

As the Pushpak circled over Ayodhya I saw all of Ayodhya on the streets; in the last fourteen years I hadn't seen more than ten people together at one time. I couldn't stop smiling, that past was behind, the future yet to come, but today was here and I was back in Ayodhya!

As Ram stepped out of the Pushpak there was a burst of crackers and all of Ayodhya started clapping, I am sure the heavens must have reverberated with the sound. Sumantra was waiting with the chariot, the very same chariot that took us to the banks of the Tamsa River fourteen years ago. He was so overcome with emotion he jumped off the chariot and just hugged Ram and me. Dear Rishi Vashistha then came forward, tears of joy streaming from his eyes; he had greyed since I last saw him. The entire court was there to receive us, I recognised everybody, many whom I had not even thought of in the last so many years. Then an ascetic stepped forward, Bharat! Ram gasped, we knew he had taken the vows of an ascetic yet we were all taken aback at to see him in the ochre robes of an ascetic.

Ram and I then got into the chariot and we drove to the palace. I was reminded of my marriage procession; it was much the same, yet much more. The much loved King of Ayodhya had returned and the people pulled off all stops to celebrate. Arches of banana leaves had been erected along the route, colourful banners fluttered from the lamp posts; the people cheered and showered us with flower petals as we passed them.

We were welcomed at the main door by Mother Kaushalya, Mother Sumitra and Queen Kaikeyi. I noticed with sorrow that since my father-in-law had passed on, the Mothers would not perform any religious ceremonies. So Shanta my sister-in-law, Urmila, Mandavi and Shrutakirti came forward to wave the lamps around us. We were meeting for the first time after the trauma we had experienced; more than happiness we felt relief! We were fourteen years older and perhaps wiser than when we parted. There was happiness on every face, however Queen Kaikeyi looked sheepish. I avoided eye contact with her. I had forgiven her but could not forget that she had been instrumental in ruining the youth of four young couples. Alas! She had won the battle but lost the war. Poor Queen Kaikeyi! What a life she must lead now.

The rituals over, Urmila, Mandavi, Shrutakirti and I hugged each other at the same time. Urmila and Mandavi had more than one reason to be happy. They escorted me to my palace; I walked through the familiar corridors - not much had changed here. Bharat had redone our palace and as my sisters led me from room to room I could only experience their love for me, the décor of the palace was immaterial.

In the evening there would be a small ceremony officially welcoming us back home. Rishi Sringi was to conduct the ceremony and I had to be dressed for the occasion. So here I was, now playing my part in the palace, only this time it was the role of the Queen of Ayodhya.

When I reached my room I found a huge pile of new sarees laid out, "What are these?" I asked.

Urmila said, "After the one year of mourning for our father-in-law was over, Mother Kaushalya decided that life must go on and we would continue our traditions and celebrate every festival. Ram, Seeta and Lakshman will be back soon and we are no longer in mourning. On every festival a new saree was bought for all of us and the Mothers insisted that we wear them and these are yours".

"What will I do with so many sarees?" I said.

Urmila looked at me perplexed, "What is with you Seeta, you loved collecting sarees, you always had more sarees than me or mother. What did you do with them then? You are now the Queen of Ayodhya you will need these and more."

Mandavi said, "The people like their queen to be better dressed than anybody else."

"For fourteen years I subsisted on the bare minimum and suddenly I see so much. There are many who don't even have a second saree which they can wear when the first is washed and here is a pile of sarees and I don't know which one to wear". I said. The three couldn't comprehend what I was saying. They did not see life from my perspective; I didn't blame them - they had always lived in the palace and hadn't seen the world. I sighed; it would take me time to get used to my old life with a new perspective.

Mother Sumitra arrived and ordered Urmila and Mandavi to go back to their palaces where their husbands would arrive shortly. Shrutakirti and Mother Sumitra helped me get dressed for the ceremony. Having got unused to the ways of the palace I was rather clumsy and forgot that the maids-in-waiting would do everything and I just had to stand and instruct them. So I got in their way, tripped over my saree and was out of my depth. The maids were patient but Shrutakirti burst out laughing. Suddenly the composed Mother Sumitra dissolved in tears; now what is it I thought to myself. She wiped her tears with the end of her saree and said "We take life for granted, and we never even think of thanking God for all that he has given us. We thank Him for the big things in life, but, I for one have never thanked Him for the small things that beautify my life – this laughter for instance is music to my ears. I am so grateful to God that I have ears to be able hear laughter".

The eight of us, Shanta and the three mothers came together in the evening for the ceremony. Rishi Vashistha, Sumantra and their wives Arundhati and Bhagirathi were the only others present. Ram, Lakshman and Bharat looked so different - they had changed out of their ascetic robes. Oh, so this was how Ram looked before we went into the forest, what a handsome man, I mused.

Shanta then put coconut, fruits and uncooked rice grains, all symbols of fertility, in the laps of Urmila, Mandavi, Shrutakirti and myself; she blessed us with progeny to take forward the Raghu Dynasty.

Lakshman and Urmila looked a little uncomfortable with each other; they behaved as if they were meeting for the first time! My husband noticed this and after the ceremony was over, told Lakshman that he did not want to see him for one month after the coronation which was the next day. Bharat was told that he would spend a few hours in the morning with Ram after which he should not be seen around. He instructed Mother Kaushalya that the four were not to be sent for without his permission. Ram said to me, "They must spend time together". How sensitive it was of him to think of them in this manner!

Ram came to me and said that he would like it for both of us to go and pay our respects to Queen Kaikeyi. I did not want to argue with Ram, so I nodded without meeting his eye and engaged myself in a conversation with Shanta, Ram's older sister. The rigid code of conduct of the Raghu Dynasty came to my rescue. Shanta had her back towards him and so didn't know he was waiting for me, I pretended not to see him and he would never interrupt when his older sister was speaking. Once Shanta started talking she would not stop, Ram waited for a while and then moved away. I saw him go towards Queen Kaikeyi's palace but didn't follow him. I had not expressed any negative emotion towards her so far, neither did I intend to in the future but I certainly wasn't going to her palace to pay my respects. When my husband was officially King of Kosala, the Queen of Kosala would acknowledge the greetings of the queen mother!

That evening Ram brought up the issue with me, I said to Ram, "Ram, rules are made for man; sometimes I feel that you believe that man is made for rules. I have feelings and have not reached your level of dispassion, please bear with me. I am myself first and only thereafter your wife or for that matter the Queen of Kosala. Talking of rules and Dharma, did any of the Raghus think of what the Janaks must have felt when you were preoccupied with discharging your Dharma?" Ram looked hurt; he just nodded and went out of the room. I was sorry that he was hurt but I thought I needed to convey to him that the Universe was much larger than the Kingdom of Kosala and the Raghu Dynasty.

After sunset Sumantra came to the palace and told Ram that the entire city had been lit up to celebrate our arrival and so we must drive around the city to respect the sentiment of the people and join them in celebrations – the King of Ayodhya had no choice and so we set out for a drive around the city.

It was the darkest night of the year, the night of the new moon in the month of Kartik. Hundreds of lamps lined the streets; every home was lit up to welcome the Goddess Lakshmi and Ram. Everything was familiar; what a good feeling to be home at last!

People poured out of their homes to greet us, offering us sweets and bursting crackers, there was a spontaneous outpouring of love. At some places they wanted to see Ram and at others they wanted to see me; we would step out of the chariot and receive their greetings and blessings; we returned to the palace late in the night and very tired.

The usual fare was prepared for the evening meal, the three of us, Ram, Lakshman and myself, could not bring ourselves to eat the food; we had no appetite for spices. It took us sometime to get back to eating the palace food; we had grown quite used to the "jungle fare".

When we retired to our palace for the night, Ram just could not sleep in the room, he said he was suffocating; he wanted to sleep under the stars. He tossed and turned for half the night, he finally took a mat and slept in an adjoining balcony. Aren't we creatures of habit!

Although I was very tired I couldn't sleep for a long time as well. I was pondering over the purpose of my life and the specific purpose of the forest experience.

Next morning, Ram and I rose early and walked to the Shiva Parvati temple; he had said that the sooner we come back to our routine the better it would be for all of us. On the way back I put to him the question that was nagging me all night.

Ram replied, "We all learn lessons in life particularly in times of adversity, for the Raghu Dynasty the last fourteen years have been a 'condensed course'; the challenge for all of us now is to be able to apply these lessons in our daily lives. God has infinite patience and compassion, until and unless one learns the lesson, the experience repeats itself; for unless we have learnt the lesson we are not fit to climb the next step of the ladder of evolution, and God wants us to do just that, evolve to a point where we merge with the infinite".

"As for your purpose in life, Seeta, we come into this life alone and we depart alone. Along this journey we meet parents, siblings, friends, partners and enemies, but all of them will walk only part of the way with us. Nevertheless each has an important and unique role to play, the mother's role being the most important since she has given us life. We play different roles in our lives and to each role we must give due attention. It is here that we must be able to discriminate 'how much attention to what' and prioritise on the principle –'the greatest good of the greatest numbers'. Each one of us has to determine our purpose in life, with the ultimate goal being one of merging with the infinite". In that Ram also responded to my accusation of none of the Raghus considering the hurt caused to the Janaks.

The morning after we returned, Ram was officially coronated as the King of Kosala; it was another day of celebrations. Now Ram got very busy with the affairs of the State but always found time for me. We had begun to live as any other married couple, we went for long walks together and when we couldn't go out we would play chess, our favourite game. Ram was infinitely more attentive to me now than he was before we left for the forest; he would even participate in choosing which saree I would wear for a particular occasion and the jewellery to go with it, funnily I always agreed with his choice.

While Ram was at work I would spend time with Mother Kaushalya and Mother Sumitra, our return had given them a purpose to live. I never saw Manthara on my return. I was told that age had taken its toll and she was unable to leave her bed; I felt sorry for her, but left her to herself. I now got a chance to talk to my sisters at length. When listening to my story, Mandavi would burst into tears as if she were responsible for my trials. Bharat and she kept away from Queen Kaikeyi. Like me, Mandavi had forgiven her but could not forget what she had done. I decided I was not going to interfere in that relationship, as long as decorum was maintained, and in any case Queen Kaikeyi too kept to herself.

One morning, about six months after our return Ram told me he had a surprise for me and he would bring it with him when he returned for lunch. The child in me could not wait for the surprise. I pleaded with him to tell me, he laughed, "Seeta you waited for a year for me in Lanka and now you cannot wait till the afternoon"! And off he went. I counted the hours for him to return, I asked Mother Kaushalya if she knew of the surprise, she did not answer my question but said, "Ram loves you so much, you have no idea", and so I guessed she too knew, but wouldn't tell me and this increased my curiosity and impatience all the more. When Ram returned earlier than usual I ran up to him like a little child and looked at him expectantly; he laughed, "It's coming, wait". Just then visitors were announced and in walked my parents, my uncle Kushadhwaj and aunt Ganga, I squealed in joy. I hadn't met my parents for over fourteen years and was planning to ask Ram to send me to Mithila, now they were here! Mother Kaushalya told me that this was Ram's idea; he had been burdened with guilt about the trials we four sisters had been through. He had told her he couldn't reverse anything in the past, but would do his utmost to ensure our happiness in the future.

That evening I apologised to Ram for having said he had been inconsiderate to the feelings of my parents. He said, "Seeta you were right in what you felt. But what was I to do? I was caught between a hard rock and the deep sea. I have spent sleepless nights consumed with guilt because I permitted Lakshman to come and separated him from Urmila. I wept night after night when you were in Lanka; I told myself that had I not permitted you to come, you would not have been abducted. What is more Seeta, as a husband I chide myself for having made you go through trial by fire, but I have this unenviable role of being King and husband at the same time. Remember one thing always, I love you more than anything else in the world, but sometimes I have to decide whether I am King or husband; unfortunately for you and more than that for me, my role as a King will always take precedence over my role as a husband."

A few months later I would realise that Ram's words had been prophetic. But for now, the joy of meeting my parents occupied me completely. We spent hours talking, making up for lost time. Often we were transported into the past as we recalled memories of our childhood and home. They stayed for a couple of weeks and on the eve of their departure my aunt announced that Mandavi was pregnant. There was jubilation in the family, finally some good news!

When the midwife announced the birth of a son Queen Kaikeyi gifted her a hundred gold coins. I thought it was overdoing things, after all he was not the heir apparent, my son would have the first claim to the throne. When Ram got the news, he was overjoyed and said "An heir to the throne of Kosala has arrived! This calls for celebration". I was taken aback, and it must have shown on my face because Rishi Vashistha who was present said something in a low voice to Ram and there was no further talk of celebrating the arrival of an heir to the throne of Kosala. Bharat and Mandavi's son was named Taksha.

Taksha was the centre of attraction and he was a lovely baby; his coming brought us all great happiness; this was the first piece of good news for the family in a long time. With Taksha's arrival the relationship between Bharat and his mother healed. The change that Taksha brought to Queen Kaikeyi's mood was dramatic; she was now her old self. Everybody thought it was because she now had something to distract her from her guilt, I thought differently – I had a feeling she saw in the infant the future King of Kosala. Mandavi was an amazing girl, she was not at all possessive about Taksha, she would get him ready and send him with his nanny to my palace; I loved him and eagerly awaited his arrival, but I was always conscious of the fact that Taksha was not my son.

Some months later Urmila and then Shrutakirti announced their pregnancies and there was much celebration in the palace. I was getting a little worried, it was almost two years that we had returned and I hadn't conceived; Ram did not seem to be perturbed, he would laugh away my worries and say, "You have Taksha, don't fret about not having children". I decided to speak to Arundhati, the wife of Rishi Vashistha. Not long after, I heard the Sage had gone into the Himalayas to meditate; Arundhati had not accompanied him because her favourite cow was due to deliver her calf any day. This I thought was the most opportune time when I would get her to myself. I sent a message telling her that I would like to visit her; she replied that I should come and spend an entire day with her. So off I went, Ram knew I was fond of her and was happy that I would be spending time in Rishi Vashistha's hermitage. Arundhati was tending to her plants in the garden when I arrived. She welcomed me with a warm hug and took me around the garden showing me her plants. I pretended to be interested but my attention was not entirely on the plants. She stopped mid sentence, held my shoulders and turned me towards her, "Vaidehi, what is the trouble, child?" I dropped my mask and wept, "Mother I am tired of acting. I have to appear happy, content and at peace at all times. Everybody believes that being the Queen of Kosala guarantees happiness, that is not so. Being the Queen of Kosala and being happy are two different things. What have I to be so happy about; the memories of thirteen years in the forest or the one year in Lanka? Or should I be happy about the fact that Bharat and Mandavi have produced the first son in the family. I have not been able to produce an heir for the throne of Kosala – actually let me be honest, I want my own children. Taksha is not my child, I haven't yet conceived and that is making me very unhappy."

Arundhati led me back into the hermitage and let me cry my heart out; she held me close and wiped my tears with the end of her saree, she could have been my mother. When my sobs subsided Arundhati said, "I understand your pain, child; your role is not any easy one. I am not going to tell you that it is merely a role that you are playing and that it is temporary. For us, what we experience is our reality. You have had a very difficult time, a lesser person would have broken down long back, you have held out. You are justified in crying out your sorrow, sometimes just crying washes away unhappiness, don't suppress the pain you experience, cry or talk about it. Often our behaviour tries to fit another's expectation of us, who does it help? Not us. Vaidehi for a start be 'yourself' to 'yourself'. Don't mould yourself to please others, this does not mean you should neglect your duties towards your husband or his mothers, but remember that the most important person in the world is you".

My weeping over, already I was feeling better; Arundhati had me eat fruits grown in the hermitage and gave me fresh milk. She continued with her chores and we talked. I felt so light, there were no pretences here and there was no palace politics. I sat by her and watched her cook. She cooked a simple fare of rice and some seasonal vegetables which we washed down with buttermilk. Over lunch Arundhati said to me, "Vaidehi, as a rule my husband and I do not look into the future, it is indecent to do so. By looking into the future we are intruding on the Creator's privacy[41]. But to give you solace I'll tell you what I can see, you will have sons in the not distant future but I also see you have a difficult pregnancy. Beyond that I don't want to delve". Hearing

---

[41]   Unpublished talks of Sadguru K Sivananda Murthy

that I would bear children lifted my dejected spirits, I took her leave and she promised to come someday to the palace. Arundhati had said 'sons', I was delighted, I kept this news to myself and now had something to look forward to. 'Sons', perhaps daughters would follow.....

CHAPTER 11
Beyond Ayodhya

Some months after my meeting with Arundhati I discovered I was pregnant; I shared this with Mother Kaushalya who kept it a secret till I broke the news to my husband. He was awkward at first, he didn't know how to handle the emotion of knowing he was going to be a father soon; and then he was delighted. Then he spoilt it all by saying "This child will be Shatrughna of the next generation, Taksha will be Ram of the next generation– just what did he mean; I didn't want to spoil the atmosphere by saying –Taksha may be older but my child is the heir to the throne of Kosala and so kept silent.

My first trimester brought with it morning sickness and lethargy; Ram was a very considerate husband and was very sensitive to my needs. As I overcame the morning sickness and wanted to eat sour and pungent flavours, he arrived one afternoon with a raw mango. We ate it just as we had done in the early years of our marriage; Ram broke it with the side of his palm and generously sprinkled it with red chilli powder and salt. For me that was romance!

This was a period of great happiness, there were three boys in the family now, Mandavi's Taksha, Shrutakirti's Bhupaketu and Urmila's Angad and I had announced my pregnancy. The three grandmothers had their hands full taking care of their grandsons. The nannies were only on standby! Every day we discovered a new milestone; either Taksha had articulated his first word or Bhupaketu had lifted his head or little Angad had begun to open and close his fists.

I had noted for some days that Ram was preoccupied with something; he seemed disturbed but wouldn't share it with me. One morning he said to me, "Seeta would you like to go and live in Mithila for sometime?" This was a strange question, I didn't know where it was coming from; I was pregnant, carrying the future heir to the throne of Kosala and the journey to Mithila would be strenuous so what was going on? I replied in the negative and asked Ram why he had suggested this. Ram took a deep breath and said "Let me tell you the cause of my asking you to go away from here". I was startled; he had earlier said, "Go and stay for sometime in Mithila", now he was saying, "Go away from here". I waited for him to speak and he fumbled and stammered as he said, "Some people in the city are unhappy with the fact that I continue to live with you despite the fact that you spent a whole year in the home of another man. They say that this is giving licence to women to do as they please. You know well Seeta, that I trust you completely but what I do will be an example for the others. For the sake of my people I must ask you to stay away from the palace for sometime, till those rabble rousers realise their foolishness".

Saying this Ram broke down, laying his head on my lap he wept bitterly; but I was in no frame of mind to pacify him.

The blood in my veins had run cold and my knees turned wobbly; I could not believe what I had heard – here was one of those women who I had seen in the future whose chastity was questioned. I got up unsure if my knees would carry me, but they did and I came out into the balcony for a breath of fresh air. Ram remained where he was, sobbing. I let him be where he was, so this is what he meant, I thought, when he had said, "My role as a King will always take precedence over my role as a husband".

My anger was rarely roused but today I was furious. I said to him in a voice trembling with anger, "Ram, you cannot stand up for your wife; why wife? You are not even capable of standing up for yourself; I am part of you and carry a part of you? Have we not already proved to the world my purity? You well know that I am pure, you know the child in my womb is yours, the world knows it. I have conceived this child after two years of our return from the forest. How could you even entertain this nonsense? Your idea of Dharma is that people must be allowed to express themselves. The consequences of their expression are of no consequence. Your mother, Queen Kaikeyi did that once and now some nobody makes some irresponsible statements and both times I must pay! And just for the record – I did not stay even for a night in Ravana's palace; I lived in the Ashoka Van. Moreover except for the time when he abducted me Ravana did not touch me. How dare you Ram! How dare you!"

Having vented my fury I calmly told Ram, "You have expressed your wish Oh King! It is now my Dharma to ensure that you are enabled to follow your Dharma". Ram continued sobbing and I got on with my morning routine. It was a long time before a swollen eyed Ram left for the court.

I finished my prayers and sat down to think of what I must do now. At first I thought of pleading with him, pleading to the people of Ayodhya, I was sure not everybody thought I was unchaste. Where would I go? What would I do?

Musing so, I felt my little one kick me in the stomach and then I felt another kick; it was different from the first. I was five months pregnant and much larger than what either of the girls had been when they were in the fifth month of pregnancy. For the first time I suspected I was carrying twins – hadn't Arundhati said 'sons'. The two kicks brought me to my senses.

I had been concerned about the fact that at least Ram and Queen Kaikeyi regarded Taksha as the first born. Moreover Ram's remark at the time of his coronation, "Not just they, but even their progeny will not beget this honour of becoming King of Kosala, I cannot reconcile myself to this injustice"; which had not meant anything then, now sounded ominous. Did he intend to divide the kingdom among all the children? It was unacceptable to me. Although I was quite clear about the principle of primogeniture which was followed by the Raghus – eldest male child of the eldest male would be King. Who would listen to my protests? If I were to protect my children's interests this was a God sent opportunity. My husband could forfeit his claim to the throne that was his choice; but my Dharma was to protect my children's inheritance. If Ram had made a choice between King and husband; I made the choice between mother and wife. I suppose this is what he meant by 'discrimination and priority'.

But where would I go? Going back to Videha was not an option. I did not want my children growing up as refugees in another's palace; even if it were my parental home. I wanted them to be away from the palace of Ayodhya and its influence. I was sure I wanted them to grow up as Kshatriyas and to be equipped to take on their role as Kings. Their mother would protect their rights and not accept a slice of the cake for them – the entire cake was theirs and nobody could deny it to them. I suddenly thought of Rishi Valmiki's hermitage, surely he would give me shelter.

Now that I had dismissed the need to prove my chastity and purity to the people of Ayodhya and my plan was in place, I regained my strength. My purpose in life was clear – to protect the interests of my unborn children. I was calm, I had no anger in me; in fact the dominant emotion in me was my love for Ram. I realised he had a difficult choice, but the choice was his.

That afternoon when Ram came home I informed him, "I am leaving tomorrow at the crack of dawn; please arrange a chariot to take me"

Now Ram's blood must have run cold, "Where are you going? You are heavily pregnant!" He said.

Calmly I responded, "Ram I am following your wishes; henceforth where I am going will not be known to you. As far as being pregnant, I have been pregnant for the last five months. These are my children and I shall take care of them. I will not bid farewell to the others, I leave it to you to give them a suitable explanation for my leaving". I did not give Ram a chance to continue the conversation.

The next morning I rose before day break, picked up one saree out of my large collection; one I was already wearing. I now had two sarees which would last me many years. Lakshman was waiting in the chariot. I had hoped that Ram would stop me but he did not; his expression was stony and he did not even come up to the chariot to bid me farewell. When Lakshman whipped the horses, I said to him, "Lakshman go south". I don't know what Ram must have told Lakshman, but Lakshman asked me no questions and did what I bade. We had travelled a distance and I could now see the Tamsa River in the distance. I asked Lakshman to stop and got down from the chariot. Without looking back I walked on; it was a while before I heard Lakshman turn the chariot and start his journey towards Ayodhya. When I could no longer hear the chariot I sat down on the grass and wept and bemoaned my fate. Again my children kicked me into action and I got up and began to walk towards the confluence of the rivers Ganga and Tamsa. It was early evening, the cattle were returning to their homesteads and people returning home from the village market.

A bullock cart with a farmer and his wife passed by and stopped. The wife got down and asked me what I was doing in this part of the forest all alone. "You are pregnant, lady; you look to be royalty, what sort of a man is the father of your children who has left you alone in this wilderness?" When I didn't answer the farmer said, "Well if your husband has forgotten his Dharma we have not forgotten ours. Tell us where you are bound, we'll take you there. I don't want to die with the sin of abandoning a lady and a pregnant lady at that in the forest." I only pointed in the direction of Rishi Valmiki's hermitage. "Is it to the Rishi's hermitage you want to go?" I nodded. "Come along then we too are going there." I had not had a sip of water since the morning; the wife seemed to guess, she offered me water from her pitcher. I cupped my hands and drank deeply, I must have emptied the pitcher because she then took out some dry chapattis and offered them to me, "You look hungry, but I have only these". I was very hungry and as I ate the chapattis, I thought to myself – Queen of Kosala you are destined to receive alms. Just after sunset we reached the hermitage, the farmer called to one of the disciples. "Tell the Rishi we have brought him a guest".

Rishi Valmiki seemed to be expecting me, "Come Seeta", was all he said. I was so tired I could barely walk; I collapsed on the steps outside his cottage. The sage called out to his wife, Rohini, saying, "You always wanted a daughter, here she is; she will be called Vanadevi[42], take good care of her". Vanadevi! Or Bhudevi! Goddess of this or that – was this

---

[42]   Goddess of the Forests

the fate of a Goddess? This time I did not need to tell the Rishi the circumstances of my arriving at his doorstep. In fact nobody ever asked me how I arrived at the hermitage. The Rishi, his wife and all the residents took great care of me throughout my pregnancy. Rohini had confirmed that I was carrying twins, she also said that she felt they were both boys – I recalled Arundhati's words. In the spring I gave birth to twin boys. Rishi Valmiki named my boys Luv and Kush. At the simple naming ceremony I felt sorry that my babies did not have the royal function they were entitled to, more than that I missed their father.

The twins grew up showered with much love and care. As infants they were either in the Rishi's or in Rohini's lap. As they grew older they were the darlings of the residents of the hermitage. Kush was the naughtier of the two and as soon as he started walking he would wander off and we had a time looking for him. That was when Rohini decided that they must have anklets with bells; the boys loved the bells on the anklets, they were so innocent they didn't realise that the bells they loved was the best way of tracking them down.

Once my confinement was over, I too was allotted work in the hermitage. I was happy at being occupied. What I was happiest about was that I had identified my purpose in life – protecting the interests of my children; that motivated me to live and live happily. Rishi Valmiki reminded me so much of my father that I had no desire to make contact even with my parents; my children were the centre of my life. The hermitage was so far away from the city that only somebody who wanted to meet Rishi Valmiki would come by and so I was safe, nobody would know my whereabouts.

Sometimes I wondered if I had done the right thing by depriving the children of a royal upbringing. But what was to stop the people of Ayodhya from questioning the children's parentage? My precious boys would never have got over the trauma of being rejected by their father. This was the best thing I could do for them. They were being educated in the Vedas and were taught archery by Rishi Valmiki; in time to come they would claim their right to the throne. I recalled my father saying "Your sons should be brought up to inherit the throne not by their birth alone but by their ability". I did not miss Ayodhya, I was happy and at peace here. I often thought of Ram and with much love, but never missed him; he was in the distant past.

The twins once asked me who their father was; Rishi Valmiki had warned me years earlier that I should always be prepared with an answer, appropriate to their age, for this question. I told them that their father was a great king ruling a kingdom not far from where we lived. When they had completed their education they would meet their father. My little ones were satisfied with this answer; they never asked about their father again.

One morning we had surprise visitors, the Rishi Agastya and his wife Lopamudra. They were returning to their hermitage after a visit to Ayodhya and decided to meet Rishi Valmiki. I was sweeping the front courtyard when they arrived, so there was no chance for me to hide. I prostrated at their feet, Lopamudra lifted me and hugged me, "Seeta I am so happy to see you!" "Mother I left Seeta behind in Ayodhya - I am Vanadevi", I said. "You are a Devi no matter where you are, Vanadevi; we get your message, we have not met Seeta", said the Rishi Agastya smiling. While the two Sages were engrossed in discussion Lopamudra, Rohini and I got talking as we prepared the meal.

I recalled that when I had met her years ago she had said that I was blessed since I didn't fear the unknown, I now asked her if she had an inkling of what was in store for me. Lopamudra smiled, "I didn't know the exact circumstances, child, but I did see clouds on your horizon.

"I must tell you that since you have come away Ram is miserable. He has had a statue of gold made in your likeness and he carries it with him wherever he goes. He lives an austere life, an ascetic in the palace! He told us life has no meaning without his Seeta. He said to my husband that there is no one he can talk to. People speak to the King, nobody speaks to Ram. What is more he has realised the need for his own children. He has a large heart that can accommodate many people, but others are not like him. Child, let me assure you what he did was for his people, if he had his way, he would never have let you go. There are many who advise him to take a second wife, but he will not even entertain that thought; he has said, only Seeta can be my wife."

I had thought Ram was in the distant past, but no, he remained the King of my heart. Choking with emotion I replied, "Mother, I know Ram loves me and he knows I love him more than anything else in the world. But Ram is bound by his Dharma and his duty towards his people overrides everything. I would not desire that he do anything that will come in the way of his duty. But I too have my Dharma, I have given birth to two lives and it is my duty to protect their interests. As a mother my duty towards my children overrides everything else. For a mother the principle of, 'the greatest good for the greatest number' does not apply. Even the meek cow will attack, if her calf is threatened. Just as Ram misses his own children, my boys miss a father, at the appropriate time they will be reunited."

I was not surprised that my husband had not taken another wife; he had seen the problems that polygamy brings to the throne. More than that Ram respected women and believed that polygamy was unfair to a woman. Also I knew that our love for each other would never let him admit a thought for anybody else.

Lopamudra told me that Rishi Agastya had recommended that Ram perform the Ashwamedha Yagna for the twin purposes of establishing his suzerainty in the area and for his own salvation. The Rishi and his wife stayed overnight in the hermitage; the next morning as they were setting out Lopamudra called me aside and said, "Why don't you go through the Agni Pareeksha[43] in the presence of the people of Ayodhya, establish your purity and spend the rest of your life with the man you love?". Clearly she was echoing Ram's wishes; I looked into her eyes and said, "Agni Pareeksha for what Mother? What wrong have I done, that I need to

---

[43] Trial by fire

prove myself repeatedly? I am not going to be judged by the people of Ayodhya for some whim and fancy of theirs, God above knows the truth and that's what matters at the end of the day. I sleep with a clear conscience. Others may keep their doubts. Today I am beyond the need for people to certify my purity." Lopamudra hugged me, "I like your spirit, Vanadevi; but I do wish you are reunited with Ram. God be with you".

Some years later, when the boys were about fourteen years old, they had gone off to the forest with the other students of the hermitage, to collect firewood. I was wondering what had taken them so long, when one of the boys of the hermitage came panting home; he called out to Rishi Valmiki, "Guruji! Luv and Kush have caught hold of a horse that was roaming in the forest. A huge army is following it, they say it belongs to the King of Kosala". I caught my breath, my children were very young they could not possibly challenge the army of Kosala, but Rishi Valmiki signalled to me to say nothing. Instead he said, "Go son, stand by Luv and Kush and challenge the army, come back when you have won". I was terrified! I feared for my children's life but Rishi Valmiki was very confident. "Have faith in my tutelage, I have given your sons the best training in archery, they are invincible, they will even take on their own father", he said to me.

I still feared for their safety and could not concentrate on anything I was doing. Every evening all the boys would return and tell us about the day's events. I could not sleep at night; I was so worried, but Rishi Valmiki would assure me that everything would be alright. This fight carried on for three days; on the first day the children challenged and defeated Shatrughna. On the second day they defeated Bharat, but when Lakshman was defeated I was sure Ram would come.

That evening Rishi Valmiki told the children their history but told them that their father was the King of Ayodhya not the King of Kosala. My boys who had not been exposed to the outside world did not know that Ayodhya was the capital of Kosala and accepted everything that their Guru said. The next morning Rishi Valmiki accompanied the boys. Ram did come the next day, he must have been wondering who had the temerity and ability to challenge his brothers.

That he came on foot and without his bow and quiver was a mystery to me, till I heard Rohini's explanation.

Rohini had said to me, "Does a father ever pick up arms against his children? Do you think this is the first life that Ram is their father or your husband? Parents and children, husband and wife spend many life times together. That is why there is so much attachment; it is not the love and attachment of one life but of many life times. You and Ram have been and will remain husband and wife for eternity and in every life, just as in this one, you will recognise each other. Ram did not know that it was his sons who had held his horse captive, but deep down a voice must have prompted him to act the way he did. Don't forget God is 'compassion'".

Ram stood in front of the boys and said, "Boys who are you and why did you hold my horse?" My boys replied, "Where is your bow, Oh King? Let us first settle this issue with bows and arrows and then we will tell you who we are. As for holding your horse, it strayed into our territory and so we were within our rights to take the horse captive."

Ram said, "It is against my Dharma to fight my sons and so have left my bow and arrows behind".

Luv replied to Ram, "Oh King please do not call us your sons, our father is King Ram, the King of Ayodhya. Only he may call us 'son'".

Ram was taken aback and asked the child who was their mother, Kush replied, "Naturally my mother is the wife of the King of Ayodhya, her name is Vanadevi".

Rishi Valmiki then stepped forward and told Ram that these were his very own sons. Ram stepped forward to gather them in his arms, but they refused to be hugged; "You have been unfair to our mother, how can we accept you now?" Rishi Valmiki then sent for me. I said to the boys, "He is your father. A father has the right to the greatest honour, and you must give him that honour."

Ram and I looked at each other, but this time there was no sharp current flowing between us; only a look of deep understanding of the pain we both had experienced because of separation, of love and of forgiveness for the unintended hurt we had caused each other. "Do you accept them as your sons?" I asked. How could Ram have refused? Luv was a splitting image of Ram and Kush was like me. The boys stepped in, "But we haven't finished our fight yet".

Smilingly Ram said, "There is no fight my boys and you have won! The kingdom of Kosala was always yours by right and now you have it by might!"

I closed my eyes in gratitude, I had reunited father and sons; my sons had got their inheritance by might and so it was their right. I had achieved the purpose of my life. I was no longer wife or queen, I was a mother, and a mother I would always remain and I was free to go!

As I turned and walked away I wondered if posterity would be able to understand the great sacrifices Ram had made, to set standards of behaviour for the common man. For his firm belief in "What the Raghu Race does will be cited as classic norms by folks in all ages to come" – the first time he had given up his kingdom and the second time, his wife. Would posterity ever realise that it was I who made the decisions? It was *my* decision to join my husband when he was asked to live in the forest for fourteen years; it was *my* decision to undergo a trial by fire in Lanka; it was *my* decision to leave Ayodhya for *my* sons and finally it was *my* decision not to subject myself to being judged by the people of Ayodhya!

EPILOGUE

Seeta had achieved her purpose in life; she turned around and began walking away. Ram stepped forward to call out to her, but Luv restrained him. "Father, for so long she has lived for others, if this is her choice give her the freedom she desires and deserves", he said. Surely this is Seeta's son, thought Ram – the unmistakable spark- only Seeta's off spring could have it. Ram stood rooted to the spot as he saw his beloved Seeta disappear from sight, but hadn't he asked her to disappear once? He just stood and watched he had stopped hurting years ago; by now he was accustomed to the loneliness – a space only his Seeta could have filled; truly he couldn't stop her now.

Ram turned to his boys, "Let's go back to Ayodhya", he said. Prostrating to Rishi Valmiki the three turned towards Ayodhya. The boys who had never been beyond the forests surrounding Rishi Valmiki's hermitage, were bewildered at the magnificence of Ayodhya; they had only seen huts and here in Ayodhya the streets were lined with houses of more than two storeys! The roads were wide and lined with trees and as they drove into Ayodhya in their father's chariot, the citizens bowed down to greet their father. The three entered the palace in Ayodhya and Ram took the boys to Queen Kaushalya's palace, "These motherless boys are mine, they are the heirs to the Throne of Kosala", he said. Queen Kaushalya had been waiting for this day for many years; now she gathered her grandsons in her arms and wept tears of joy. The boys were nonplussed; they didn't understand what was so special about them other than the fact that they had captured the horse and now they were with their father.

Although he was now united with his sons, Ram missed Seeta terribly. Why was life so unkind he brooded, why couldn't he and his beloved Seeta enjoy their sons? "Was I to blame?" He would ask himself over and over again – but the answer eluded him. Ram now had a cause of his own to live for; he groomed his boys to become Kings after him. He could not have faulted Rishi Valmiki for the education he had given the boys; ever so often he would see the spark of his Seeta in the boys and his heart ached. After ruling Kosala for many years, Ram decided to hand over the Kingdom to his sons. When the people heard this, they wept and tried to dissuade him, "This time I will listen to only my voice", he said. The citizens then came to him and said they wanted to put up his statue so that they may never forget him. Ram smiled, "I have been separated from my Seeta for most of my life and now if you want to remember me, always remember me with Seeta by my side". And so to this day Ram is always seen with Seeta by his side.

What Seeta feared came to be; most of the time women have to prove their innocence and their ability and Seeta's apparently unquestioning acceptance of situations and dedication to her husband is the norm for all women irrespective of the circumstances; but few follow King Ram who did his duty no matter what role he played – son, husband, friend or ruler. King Ram for whom the greatest good of the greatest number was most important; for whom being a ruler meant setting standards by personal examples, sometimes at great cost to himself.

Bibliography

Das, Tulsi. *Ram Charit Manas*, Comp. Hanuman Prasad Poddar Gita Press, Gorakhpur 12 ed. *2066 Saka Samvat*

Maharaj, Saraswati, Akhandanand. *Adhyaatma Ramayan* Comp. Somdutt Dwivedi Sahitya Prakashan Trust Mumbai 2006. Talks

K.R, Iyengar, Srinivasa. Sitayan Samata Books, Chennai 1987

Sivananda Swami Lives of Saints: Sivananda Publication League. Rishikesh 1993 Web.

Rajgopalachari, C. Ramayan Bharati Vidya Bhavan 53 ed. Mumbai 2013

Valmiki Ramayana Abr. And Trans. Arshia Sattar Penguin New Delhi 2000

Valmiki, Maharishi. Gita Press Gorakhpur

Lal, Malashri and Namita Gokhale ed. In Search of Sita Penguin New Delhi 2009

"Valmiki Ramayana." Sri Desiraju Hanumanta Rao and Sri K. M. K. Murthy
Web. 16 Dec 2013. http://www.valmikiramayan.net/.

"Did Rama Have A Sister?" *Did Rama Have A Sister?* Web. 16 Nov 2013. http://bhriguashram.org/ver3/rama_sister.php.

"Chaitra Navratri.", *Chaitra Navratra, Goddess Durga Festival of 9 Nights.* Web. 31 Mar 2014.
http://vatikashaktipeeth.com/festivals/chaitra-navaratri.html.

http://www.hindu-blog.com/